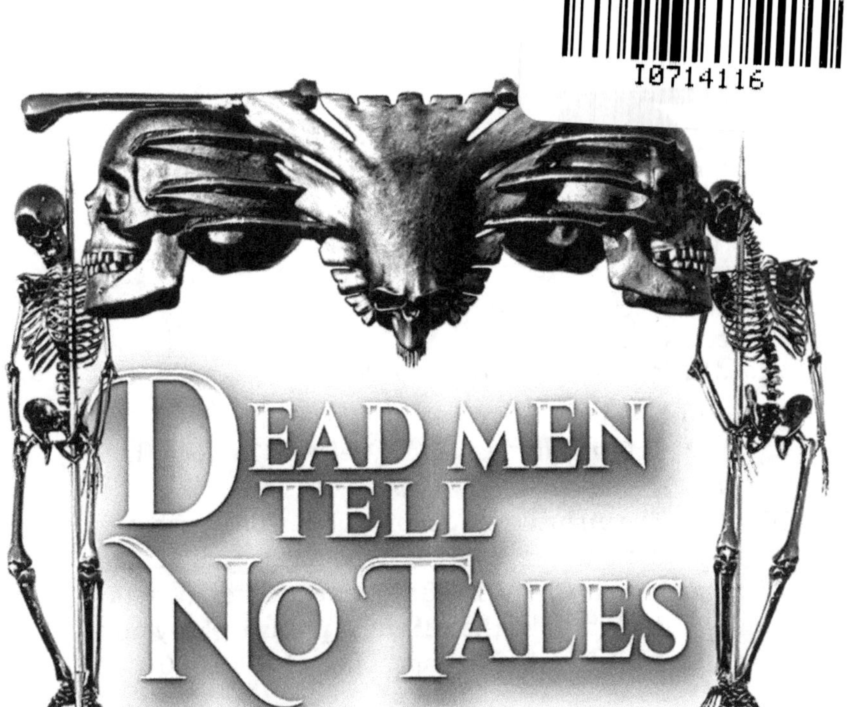

DEAD MEN TELL NO TALES

JEFFREY KOSH

GRINNING SKULL PRESS
Bridgewater, MA
USA

Grinning Skull Press

FOREWORD

The original *'Legend of the Black Schooner'* originated in the Caribbean and Spanish Main in the late 1600s to early 1700s. It also appears in written form on *'Memoirs of a Naval Man in the Caribbean'* by Captain Henry Coale. This short tale is the witness report of what happened to Port James in the year 1712.

It seems, the crew of the brig *'Anne Stuart'* stumbled on a horrible scene of death and madness in that colony; all the town's women and children had been crucified in the city square. No signs of pillaging or similar piratical activities could ever be found. All adult males were missing.

Tales of the Black Schooner had been around even earlier. They told that a pirate crew had gone adrift in the legendary Sargasso Sea. They had gone mad with isolation, and had practiced cannibalism on one another before a storm had finally set them free. It was told that they were no longer interested in booty, only for killing and eating the inhabitants of the towns they raided.

However, frontier legends from the early days of the US sometimes tell stories of mountain folk gone mad. Sawney Bean and his Scots cannibal clan still tell the urban myth of the British Isles (this story also influenced Wes Craven when he created his cannibal clan in *The Hills have Eyes*). And I bet you can find hundred of likenesses with an infamous family of chainsaw-brandishing maniacs with a taste for human flesh.

Also, these animalistic, but cunning monsters, somehow, carried to my mind the image of the *Borg of Star Trek the Next Generation*'s fame.

In fact, this legend has found its place even in space; in the movie *Serenity* (and the series *Firefly*) creatures called *'Reavers'* are clearly based on this same legend, yet with a scientific explanation. If you are a fan of the franchise, you know what I'm talking of.

I was charmed by this story, so horrific, so raw.

For what I know, the *Black Brig* is still out there. Its monstrous sailors, dressed in garments of human skin sewn into their flesh and stained with human blood, upholding their endless voyage across the sea. The sailors do not speak. They go about their grisly business with no regard for any cry of mercy. They torture the women and children. No one survives. They take the men. Some end in their larders, hung in rows, impaled on hooks through the throat. Some get press-ganged into joining.

They don't talk — they can't, having no tongues — and don't stop. They come and go with no rhyme or reason.

Jeffrey Kash

Dead Men Tell No Tales

Dedicated to my Faithful Readers.
You know who you are

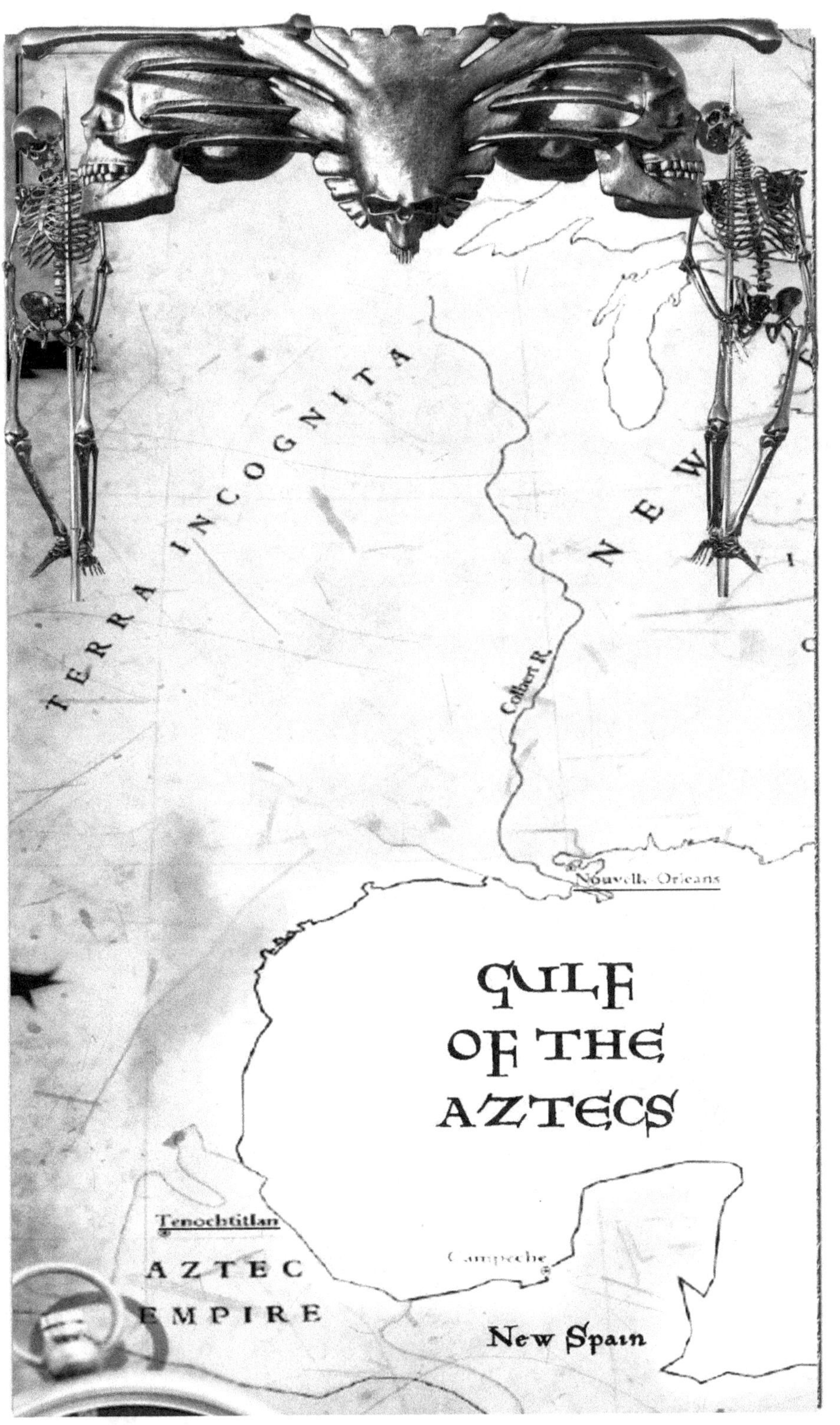

TERRA INCOGNITA
NEW
Colbert R.
Nouvelle Orleans
GULF OF THE AZTECS
Tenochtitlan
AZTEC EMPIRE
Campeche
New Spain

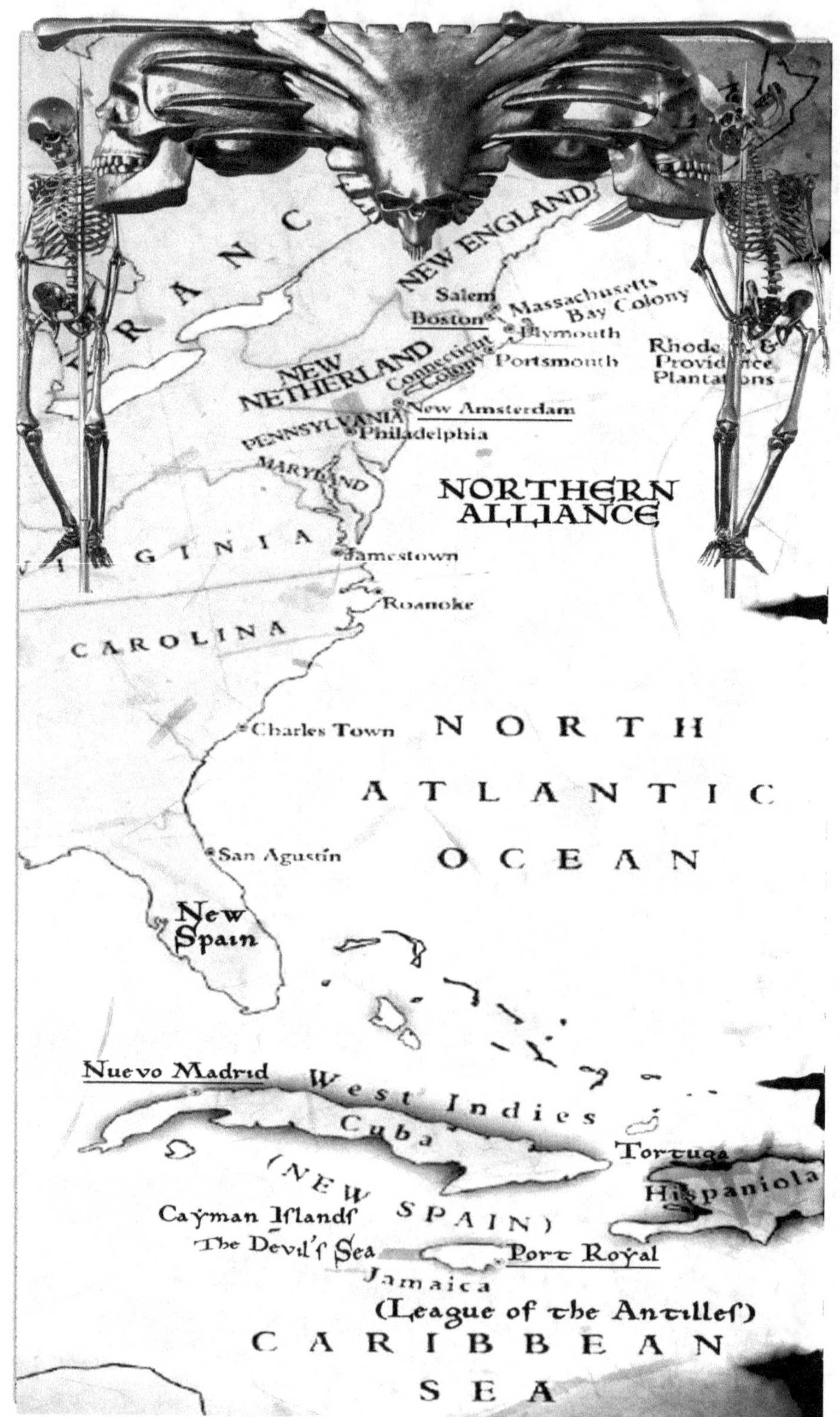
FRANCE
NEW ENGLAND
Salem
Boston
Massachusetts
Bay Colony
Plymouth
Rhode I. &
Providence
Plantations
NEW
NETHERLAND
Connecticut
Colony
Portsmouth
PENNSYLVANIA
New Amsterdam
Philadelphia
MARYLAND
NORTHERN
ALLIANCE
VIRGINIA
Jamestown
Roanoke
CAROLINA
Charles Town
NORTH
ATLANTIC
OCEAN
San Agustín
New
Spain
Nuevo Madrid
West Indies
Cuba
Tortuga
(NEW
Hispaniola
SPAIN)
Cayman Islands
The Devil's Sea
Port Royal
Jamaica
(League of the Antilles)
CARIBBEAN
SEA

NOW

1708 AD

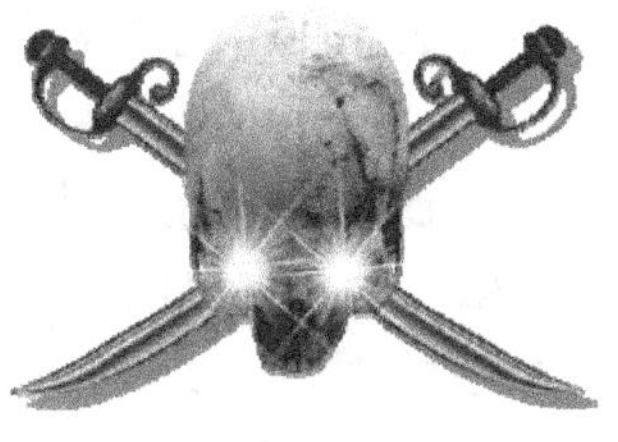

PROLOGUE

THE BLACK GULL

Scurvytown, Port Royal, Jamaica.

Life on the *Account* was filled with danger, and those who made their living on the high seas were often hardened people with nothing to lose— except their life, and large cravings.

Sailors were paid at trip's end, so they often blew away the entire wage in their shore leave. Nevertheless, there was no way to spend it aboard ship, and one never knew whether their next journey could be their last. Better make good use of all that gold rather than having it weigh you down into *Davey Jones' Locker*—the bottom of the sea. Swabs, scurvy dogs, bilge rats, and true buccaneers had no hesitation when time came to squander their loots; the taverns and brothels of Port Royal became their haunts first and foremost.

The richest favored those dives lining the narrow thoroughfares of the docks, where food was the heartiest and whores the prettiest.

The desperate stuck with Scurvytown's wretched dens of scum, where food was barely edible and the whores...well, you couldn't tell if they were members of the opposite sex.

Scurvytown was officially labeled as the 'Privateer Quarter', yet no one off the boat used that name. They reserved it for the whole dockside part of town, separating it from the 'Toffs Quarter', meaning the genteel district, where '*landlubbers*' or respected merchants made their home. The unmapped borders of Scurvytown were generally located on the east end of the harbor. The place earned its nickname by the decrepit condition of its squalid tenements, the huge transient aggregation, poverty-stricken inhabitants, and the ample spread of diseases. Brawls and bobbing bodies in the harbor were common sights, as well as the loud carousing of drunken rogues of the vilest sort.

Scurvytown was the place for those that had given up, or had no other place to go, squashed together by the same fate—that of the losers. They spent their time wasting away, unwilling to crawl up from the pit of squalor they had fallen into, dreaming about their past, brooding on their present, and dreading the future. Most of these squatters survived by doing an odd job or another by day, and ending up spending the few coppers by night in taverns and inns. The vast majority of these dens were decaying wooden buildings that hadn't seen repairs or maintenance in decades, often dug out from old warehouses, and they showed it.

One of such places was the *Black Gull.*

It took its name from a huge raven the first owner, Willie Jameson, used to keep as a pet. One night, a sailor who was so drunk he didn't know where he was, looked up from his empty mug and said, "Avast! That's th' blackiest an' ugliest gull me deadlights have ever seen!"

Immediately, Jameson renamed the bar and replaced the sign out front with a painting of the bird. A fixture in Port Royal, the tradition of keeping a raven as companion by the *Black Gull*'s owners never died, and the actual one, Angus McReady, had a large specimen named *Bean.*

The *Black Gull* was the *punch house* young officer Robert J. Higgins was looking for. Not to quench his thirst, or to find warm company for the night. No, this young fellow was looking for his new captain. Come tomorrow, he would embark on a special mission for the League, acting as liaison officer for the *Revenge,* one of the sturdiest warships in the fleet. Still, even as an agent of the Council, he knew nothing of the mission's nature, something that had clearly upset him. How could he perform efficiently if he didn't know the goal? Being a dutiful and respectful officer, Higgins never questioned his superiors, even when they clearly showed lack of experience and common sense. Nonetheless, he had enough brains to know this time it was different. There was no actual secrecy in the mission, just laziness on the part of Commodore Brian Addams. That big pig was the shame of the League's fleet, having bought his rank and position with large sums of money. A notorious epicurean, Addams spent more time at orgies than at planning ship's rosters and assignments. Robert was almost sure his name had been picked randomly from a list. Not for skills or good conduct, but out of pure chance. Knowing this in his heart, Higgins had opted for an innocent investigation, and instead of wasting away his evening at futile pleasures, he had spent some coins on snitches to locate his captain-to-be. He wanted to know the man he was going to serve before feeling the *Revenge*'s decks under his feet.

He knew his standing and strived to stick by the rules. Rules were made to be followed, as doing different would lead to anarchy, and anarchy was just the threshold to chaos. And Robert Higgins hated chaos. So, his impact with Port Royal's wild nature had immediately been a negative one.

Even worse was the *Black Gull*.

The place was rowdy, smelly, and wet. Carousers were singing old mariners' chanteys by the fireplace, and a quartet of evil-looking ... 'privateers' ... was playing cards surrounded by a small crowd of excited onlookers. Scarcely clad wenches rounded the tables, dodging some probing hands, yet welcoming others. Yes, if Port Royal was the wickedest city in the New World, the *Black Gull* was its main cathedral, from whose pulpit the verb of debauchery was spread.

Higgins scoured the place, looking for the man Peg-Paw Milton, a street informer in Scurvytown, had described to him. And found him seating in a darkened corner, his feet resting on the table while he seemed to be dozing away under the brim of his tricorn hat.

The young officer made his way with disgust amidst the crowd of smelly rogues, lifting a perfumed handkerchief to his sensible nose more than once.

"Excuse me, sir?" he hazarded almost in a whisper, fearful to cause a rude awakening to his future master. Yet, the large man didn't move. "Captain?" he insisted, this time a bit louder.

"Aye, me lad, have a seat next to me and listen to the true story of the *Banshee's Cry*," the older man said, addressing him without moving an inch. The chap wasn't sleeping.

Hesitantly, Higgins tried to introduce himself, but the burly, and rather unkempt, man shooed him instantly. "No need for presentations, lad. Just listen to me story and pay me some hearty company this night."

Peculiar. Quite peculiar, Higgins thought. Surely, the man was drunk, but he also was as alert as a weasel. Better to play by his rules.

"You know the *Banshee's Cry* legend, do you?"

Higgins replied with a hint of disbelief as he rested his back on the nearby stool. In every tavern around the known world, there were dozens of people claiming to know details of what had happened at Cayman Brac. All of them were just calling for attention, or to gain confidence on greenhorns like him. Higgins was disappointed his soon-to-be captain could be another of those braggarts. He gave the oldster a disbelieving look.

"Aye. I know the legend 'cause I have seen it meself. I was there when the Plague ended once for all," the captain insisted.

****

The captain studied the intruder, evaluating his dress and manners.

All the same, these young landlubbers, coming on the account with star-crossed eyes, dreaming of adventure in this age of rebirth. They envisioned the growing war between the Northern Alliance and the League of the Antilles as a quick way to glory and wealth, yet they knew nothing of how this New World came to be, nor of those who had sacrificed their own lives to build it. And mostly, they ignored the Plague's truth. They curled their nose at the smell of Port Royal alleys and docks, forgetting about the pleasant fragrance the sea carried on westerly winds. Because they had not lived in a world perpetually immersed in rot and decay.

"Sir, go on. I'm curious. You say you were there," mouthed the young mariner eyeing the small wooden chest resting under the man's feet, "but where, exactly?"

The captain gazed at him intently, then gulped down a draft from his mug. "*Mabouya's Well*," he said, almost whispering, that simple word still sending a shock down his spine. Even after all these years, he couldn't shake off that ghastly sensation.

"*Mabouya's Well*? Never heard about it, sir. What's this? A place in the *Devil's Sea*, a cay? Or..." Higgins hazarded, "a tavern?"

The old mariner pierced the boy with steel-gray eyes. "Blimey! Ain't believing me, ain'tcha? Fine, keep listening to bilge scum the Roundheads pump every day into the Recovery Effort. Come the morrow, bucko, you'll be pumping water yourself from the *Revenge*'s belly. Avast! Listen to me story and I promise you'll see with your deadlights the proof of what me talking."

He rejoiced at the sight of shock on the lad's face. Yes, he knew who he was and why he was here. Time to give the greenhorn a lesson about old seadogs.

However, the foppish boy didn't flinch; he kept his countenance, then straightened his back. "With all due respect, sir, I do not trust the Puritans. That's why I left New Hampshire colony and joined the Southern Royalists. Before discovering the ruse behind false promises," exclaimed the boy, his usually fine skin turning red by rekindled memories.

A smirk formed on the captain's face. Yeah, the lad was bold, maybe a bit stiff, but he could see he was the right one for the job at hand. He would fight valiantly. "Belay it, lad. Go to the bar and have this jug filled again. Then, I'll tell you a tale so grisly and scary you ain't going to sleep for months. And you be wary, 'cause the ghosts of those times still haunt us today, no matter what the Northerners say. The *Marauders* aren't a bunch of crazies, and the *Black Brig* still plies these waters."

"The *Black Brig*? A fairy tale?" Higgins exploded, clearly disappointed, then he recalled his position and quickly apologized to his commanding officer. Or at least his mouth did, for his eyes didn't. "At your command, sir. I'll fill your mug."

The boy was about to leave for the bar when the older sailor's hand reached out and grabbed his coat's cuff. "No need for that. Lissen." He invited the youngster to sit down. "Aye, this is a legend. Yet, this is also true. 'Cause that ship sailed under a different name once. Her name was *Banshee's Cry*, and she was a fine ship. She was … my ship."

THEN

1676 AD

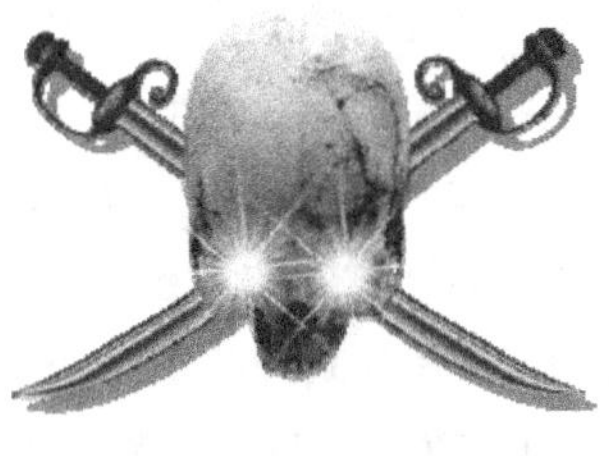

CHAPTER ONE

THE SANTA ESMERALDA

25 Miles off the coast of Inagua

"Bring her about handsomely, now!" Captain Drake shouted to be heard above his boarding crew's cries. Smoke engulfed the prow of the Banshee's Cry, as the brig came closer to the wounded Spanish merchantman.

"Avast! Moor that pregnant sow before she goes adrift," echoed MacTavish below, snapping curses in Gaelic. Drake looked amused at his boatswain. MacTavish had been with him since the beginning. An almost gnomish creature, with ash colored hair crowning a childlike face, Mac—as everybody called him—had a direct and honest personality and everyone respected him for this. He was now manning the planks with Luther, the hulking German gun master.

The Spaniard merchantman—the *Santa Esmeralda*—was a large three-masted trade vessel. Although well armed, the ship had easily fallen prey to the smaller and maneuverable brig. Its crew however had refused to surrender even after the *Banshee's Cry* had released a full load of volleys to the transport, killing most of his crew belowdeck. They were now crowding the main deck ready to stand for a final defense. Their Captain, Marcelo Salazar, was among them, trying to keep a noble countenance, but clearly shivering in his foppish leggings.

"It makes no sense, Drake," shouted Mac. "Why are they fighting?"

"Ask 'em when we are in residence. Mac," he snapped, then rushed to the castle followed by the boatswain's laughs. "I just may, Cap'n."

Drake swung from a rope directly between the two vessels, and landed his boots on the deck, then ran his cutlass through a man, drew a pistol from the fresh-made corpse and shot another with the dead man's flintlock.

At that, a swarm of fierce fighters, seasoned by years of battles, flooded the larger vessel, and the ocean filled with the clangor of blades and the sharp sound of released shots.

Handsome, in a wild fashion, Daniel 'Drake' Davies had clearly seen better days. His curly black hair, steel-gray eyes, olive-tanned skin, and robust nose revealed his Spanish blood; features he had inherited from his Andalusian mother. Daniel's father was an English fisherman from Jersey Island and this was reflected in the tall cheekbones framing his face. An unkempt and wiry beard covered most of his chin and jaw. On his neck dangled five different medallions, all coming from different parts of the world. A wooden bead necklace from Africa and a leather cord fastened to a tiny satchel from New England's natives. Another held a small metal cross from Spain, and piece of string tied to a shark tooth hailed from the Caribbean Sea. Last, a thin chain from which swung a Chinese coin. Circling his right bicep was an intricate armband made of crocodile hide, with two inlaid small teeth of the same beast. Drake had received it in his last trip to St. Lucia from a Carib, as a gift for helping him escape the clutches of a sadistic Frenchman who liked to skin natives alive.

A voice reached him. "Captain Drake. Face me."

He turned and smiled at the foppish figure wielding a well-crafted rapier. The Spaniard captain. It seemed courage had returned to him at once. "*Capitan* Salazar, *por favor*, there ain't need for bloodbath. Call back your dogs and this will be—." Drake dodged a swing from a mariner's sword, then, quickly, plunged his own blade in the assailant's throat, "—over quickly," he concluded, then booted the body from his blade.

"No. *A la muerte!*" Salazar raised his rapier in the traditional salute of duelists.

"This is stupid, *hermano*. Just surrender and we'll bring you to Port Royal, where you'll be free to pick your destiny not your ..." Drake never finished, as the Spaniard released a battle cry and thrust his pointed blade straight to his heart, forcing the pirate to jump backward to avoid the lethal strike. He rolled his eyes, grinned, tossed away the spent pistol, and wiped his cutlass on the dead body. "Well, *hombre*, you looked for it."

Blades flashed so quickly the eye couldn't follow as the two swordsmen exchanged blows, feinted, and parried with such mastery that soon, both the pirates and the merchantman's sailors stopped fighting to watch the incredible show.

"I was trained by Alonzo Mendoza in person," Salazar said while spinning on himself and tracing a small cut on Drake's already scarred face. "My family spent a fortune."

Drake jumped sideways, grabbed the opponent's cloak, and then yanked it, causing the Spaniard to lose his balance while he kicked him hard in the butt. The cloak tore off suddenly and Salazar fell facedown, his rapier escaping his hand.

"Really? A rum-sponge named Pete taught me. It cost me one doubloon and a night with the prettiest whore in Toffs Quarter." Drake kicked Salazar's rapier away while he pointed the cutlass at the man's nape.

Yells filled the deck as Drake's men saluted his triumph, yet he cut it short.

"Ahoy, mateys! Follow the rules and nobody will be hurt. We're not here to kill the crew of this floating barrel; we just want your gold. So, please, line up and collaborate with me lads. Do not, and as sure as me name's Drake, I'll have you pay a visit down to Davey Jones' Locker. And I mean the bottom of the sea," he announced, then to underline it, raised his hand and released a shot from the Salazar's own pistol.

The sailors seemed to understand, because they immediately formed a line and extended their hands forward. Drake's eyes ran to his loyal boatswain and a smirk formed at the corner of his mouth when he met the little man's eyes: he was glaring. They had made a bet, the day before, that Drake wouldn't be able to refrain using that line about Davey Jones' Locker, for he always did after capturing a chase. And Drake had clearly lost.

Meanwhile, the rest of the boarding party busied themselves getting down to the hold, eager to put their craving hands on the precious cargo. After so many days spent on the cramped *Banshee's Cry*, the merchantman seemed enormous, and its belowdecks like the dungeons of a Donnish prison. Yet, the *Santa Esmeralda* was nothing compared to the great galleons that used to ply these very waters before the Plague. The legendary prize-ships of the Spanish fleet used to cart gold and silver from the Spanish Main to the crown back in Spain. Those gargantuan cows could reach sixty yards in length and twenty yards on the beam, with a tonnage of more than two-thousand. But they were a rarity nowadays as there was no more the need to carry cargo back to defunct Spain. Gold just traveled from the Main to *Nuevo Madrid*, in Cuba.

Nuevo Madrid. Just the thought of that infernal place sent shivers down Drake's spine. It was rumored the place was one of the strangest sights in the whole world. The Spaniards, far from being in decline, as the Northern Alliance's propaganda said, were busy building something more akin to ants than to Christians. Tall tales were spoken of a city built like a beehive, a truly immense many-layered structure, reaching high into the sky, whose tapering peak consisted of the King's palace, also doubling as the center of Catholic worship in the New World. For the King of Nueva España was also the Pope of the Holy Roman Church, and his innumerable lackeys, bootlickers, and ... concubines shambled inside the dark corridors of *El Trono de Dios*—as the King's palace was known—like mindless drones. It was said the entire city was built like a hollow cone, and people from all over the world crowded it from level to level. Yet, there were also tales of engineering marvels, and incredible machineries, as whispers abounded that the artisans of *Nuevo Madrid* had harnessed the power of the steam. Nevertheless, all this industry had caused the area surrounding it to be reduced to ash wastes. So, like terrible *anthills*, swarms of thralls of the Crown streamed out of the gigantic mound to feed the endlessly hungry forges, making of *Nuevo Madrid* a reverse *Dante's Inferno.*

The sun colored the horizon in orange strokes as it set down when Geist the albino, manning the

Banshee crow's nest, issued an unexpected shout, snapping Drake out of his cerebrations.

"Sail Ho!"

Drake bolted to the rails, releasing his hold on the Spaniard captain, his eyes squinted at the sea, yet seeing nothing. Mac put immediately the glass at his eye, scanning the distance. "Shiver me timbers," he muttered, handing the tool to Drake. "Risen!"

Drake looked through the spyglass, and what he saw chilled his blood.

Huge holes gaped on the approaching *Slaver* and rotten boards jutted randomly from the sides. The foremast's top was broken off, and lay on the warped deck, amid dangling and trailing bits of ropes. Yet, what scared him most was not the sailing derelict itself, but the crew manning it.

Dressed in filthy rags, they were horrible to behold. Rotting away, yet, somehow still holding whole, with strands of algae entangled in their hair or hanging from their gnashing mouths. Bony and thin limbed they were, belying their powerful nature. Rubbery, dead-cold flesh, crisscrossed by innumerable wounds, hung loose from visible bones. Some were missing an arm or leg, but many had replaced them with other instruments. There, he could spot a blade jutting out from the stump of a burned forearm. Another had three sickles protruding as wicked claws. And axes, cutlasses, pitchforks, knives. Even more ghastly seemed the unholy decorations dangling from their very putrid skin. Severed fingers, ears, and toes had been employed by the hellish horde like earrings and bracelets. Notable among them were the truly hideous mutations; the so-called *Hullghouls*. Their bodies stood twisted in the extreme, with hairless leathery skin and evil talon-like claws. Their oversized, slobbering mouths were filled with razor-sharp teeth, made to rend flesh from bone, and their sick bodies were covered by unnatural pustules and bulging veins.

"All aboard!" Drake shouted. "Leave ship now! Whoever lingers shall be left here, hurry up!" He meant it. As cruel as it could sound, there was no other way. You couldn't kill the living dead, because they were dead already. Yes, you could delay them by chopping off their limbs, but it was impermanent. The only way to put them down for good was to destroy their brains. And that wasn't an easy task.

In addition, they carried the Plague.

It had all started ten years before, in now fallen England. Survivors said the Plague was brought into Southampton by the *Sea Venture*, a Navy frigate captained by Robert H. Hackett. Nobody knew where the crew had caught that unholy disease. Besides, none cared; they were too busy evacuating the Old World when they had realized it was not possible to contain it. When the Risen crew had shambled out the docked vessel, causing horror among the inhabitants, they were dealt with by the city militia, at least it seemed so. Then, the fiend bodies had been piled and set to flame, which cremated their cursed flesh to cinders. But soon, the dead from cemeteries and lonely graves began to rise, and people showed symptoms of the Plague. By Christmastime, it had reached London. Not even the Great Fire had stopped it. In less than five months, the Plague had spread to mainland Europe, killing off thousands of people and reanimating as much to this evil mockery of life.

Some said it was not a disease, but God's wrath, unleashed on mankind for his sins. Christians had flocked to churches, locking inside, endlessly praying the Lord to save their souls in the upcoming Apocalypse. Others blamed the foreigners, or the women, or cats, or rats, or whatever came to their blurred minds.

And everything Drake knew was lost.

Somehow, the Plague had not fallen on the New World—nobody knew why. Still, no one cared. The exodus from the Old World had been a messy affair, in which anarchy had reigned more than civil manners. Bribes and weapons insured survival to a higher degree than royalty and clerical influence did, and the New Word became a place for the merchant, not for the noble.

For years, what was left of humanity was busy at eking out a new existence in a pristine, yet alien land. New dangers and challenges were paired to new marvels and experimental societies, as the

Europeans had tried to adapt and thrive. The most powerful royalties had desperately fought to hold their status quo in the colonies, like England and Spain, but others had fallen to anarchy and civil war. New kingdoms were born, and unbelievable alliances were formed, such as The *Directorate of New England* and the *Kingdom of Nouvelle France* pact. Then, wars had started again. For human nature never changes.

Wars were fought over ideologies, resources, even women. And when it seemed the reign of the human race had reached an end in this world, out of the blue had emerged the *Northern Alliance.* With the might of combined armies and advanced firearms—mostly due to the expertise of Chinese engineers—it had quickly engulfed and subdued the surrounding barbaric warlords. Soon, the powers that be decided that all colonies should unite under their rule. And again, there was some disagreement on that point.

A War for Unification started, causing a literal exodus to the independent colonies of the Caribbean Sea. Well, they didn't find a promised land here, for it was already wracked by civil war and piracy. In the League, a ship could bring you a job as an independent. But only a gun could help you keep it.

Six months ago, the first Risen vessel had been spotted near Hispaniola. There had been questionable attacks on small settlements and tiny colonies previously, yet the League blamed rogues, royalists, and the dreaded Alliance Peacekeepers. However, these bloodthirsty attacks left no survivors, and carried away none of the booty from their nightly raids.

Except people.

Raided villages appeared desolate and silent to those unfortunate berthing their ship in these dead places.

Then, the smell of decay had settled in, forever lingering as an evil taint.

Now, the Risen were approaching quickly, driven by unnatural winds. God only knew how it was possible for that wreck to float, let alone to veer and sail. Yet, it changed tack with swiftness, as would a monstrous shark giving chase to a tasty morsel.

"Leave ship now!" Mac outcried, desperately trying to have his mates abandon the boarded freighter. Drake was already at the tiller, frantically shouting orders to the crew, his gaze frozen on the incoming monstrosity.

"In the name of God, do not leave us here!" Captain Salazar pleaded, all hostility forgotten, running to the planks and grabbing Luther's arm. The hulking German didn't flinch; he got loose of the hold and punched the Spaniard so hard he fell overboard. At that sight, chaos ensued and more than ninety men hurried toward the smaller brig, recklessly pushing everyone on their path, fighting to reach the intact vessel's safety.

"Come off it," Drake ordered, eyeing the

tattered sails. "Make speed. Bring her about!"

The *Banshee's Cry* maneuvered away from the *Santa Esmeralda*, causing most of the boarding mariners to plunge down in the frothing waters, while others clung to the keel, yet these too were easily dealt with by the pirates.

"God forgive us," muttered Mac, taking hold of the helm.

Drake nodded, but he knew there was no other choice. The brig had place for seventy men and twenty passengers; there was no space for all those people. He allowed himself a last view of the doomed freighter, before taking his decision. "Make for the Caicos."

Mac nodded and shouted, "Ready about!" And all the hands hurried to their duties.

****

Later, they took advantage of strong wind to gain distance from the ship of the dead.

Seen from a distance, the *Banshee* was beautiful to behold. Her sails were drawn in the morning zephyr as she cut a swift whooshing trail through the sparkling waters.

On board the brig, however, the image was different. Fighting men, brooding and wounded, shoved for space in the cramped ship. Their moral floundered; arguments easily broke off at every opportunity. These men had fought for nothing. They had come so close to sinking their hands in

Indian gold, only to be yanked back by the arrival of that monstrosity.

Geist scanned stern-side, figuring to spot the tattered canvases at any moment. But the dead were not giving chase, and he knew why; they were busy capturing the stranded Spaniard crew. Tavern tales said the Risen ate the living.

He knew better.

The fiends had no need for eating or drinking. Nay. They liked their victims alive, to abuse and torture 'em for days, feeding from the pain they caused. They only wished to spread the Plague, until only Death would reign. It was told they could only move in the dark, as sunlight made them drowsy, so their ship's interior was kept in pitch black darkness where they mulled about waiting for the hated sun to go down.

Geist, born Sven Haralson, was a new addiction to the *Banshee*'s crew. Tall and gangly, he looked like one of those wretched creatures, more similar to a dead than a living being, with his stark white straight, long hair and sunken eyes the color of polar ice. More than an experienced sailor gave him a wide berth, for they chilled just by looking at him. They said he was born of the Devil. Or that he was a vampire, for he loathed sunlight and was mostly active by night. He was rarely accepted aboard pirate ships, and everywhere he went, silence reigned.

But Captain Daniel Drake was different. He had noticed the man's keep vision and excellent marksmanship. Ignoring all protests from Mac, he had welcomed him on the *Banshee's Cry*. And he had never disappointed his captain. Geist could see better than anyone in the darkness. More than once, Drake had gotten his ship through shoal water and dangerous reefs with Geist on the forecastle. So, it was natural Drake trusted Geist's eyes to spot the fiend's sails in time.

In the morning, they tacked southward, entering the Windward Passage between Cuba and Hispaniola. The sea was rough and winds came and went, yet the *Banshee* performed well, and by the next dawn, they spotted Tortuga on the portside. They continued on, never stopping to founder ship in a safe harbor, too fearful of being ambushed by the undead.

Five days later, they arrived in Port Royal with a sundered mood, and an empty hold.

As the *Banshee* made her way to the docks, Drake knew that within moments there would be gunshots and celebrating yells from the population, as the arrival of a privateering ship always signaled prosperity and trade.

Yet none came for them.

CHAPTER TWO

RED LEG

Port Royal, Jamaica

It was the cackling sound of Nero's croaks that woke him up from the deep slumber he had fallen into. Otherwise, Drake would have slept the whole day, wily scoundrels allowing.

Nero was the pet raven of Willie Jameson, the owner of the *Black Gull*.

He opened an eye, and immediately regretted it. The sun was too bright for his dizzy head, the fumes of last night's carousing playing wickedly with his senses. He tried to sit up, but realized that something heavy was blocking his movements. He panicked, then noticed the reddish ringlets of hair sheathing his neck and shoulders and smirked.

That had to be Justine, the whore he had spent the night with.

Pain pierced through his weary mind as he took in his surroundings. He was lying on one of the *Black Gull*'s mangy beds in the bunkrooms on the second floor.

He shoved the prostitute off his belly and stood slowly, going for the window, where that noisy black pest perched. The girl moaned something unintelligible under her breath—a French curse, probably—then continued her slumber. At his approach, the raven flew away, cackling again, elegantly swooping down to reenter the building by the main floor.

"Damn you, matey," Drake mumbled, then took a deep intake of the harbor's late morning air.

Travelers from gentler parts of the world could delight in the delicious smell of freshly cooked seafood, seasoned with countless spices. Yet, they would retch at the rank stench of port waters, rotting fish, rubbish, and offal, which permeated Scurvytown's shabby moorings.

For Drake, a seasoned seaman, it smelled like orchids and roses if equated to the ripe stink of a Royal Navy's brig.

That was the perfume of freedom, the smell of liberty.

Drake loved Port Royal. Where in the world could you find a place as individualistic and unbound to rules as the buccaneer's town?

He also liked the sounds of the place. The city was never quiet, humming with the commotion of arguments, the cacophonic chorus of rickshaws rolling over cobbled streets, the screeches of alley cats blending with the constant snap of the vessel's flags. And most of all, the crash of the surf against the dock's bulwarks.

Next, came the wind.

There was always a breeze in the city, whistling constantly as it journeyed through the narrow and twisted streets, carrying the smell of sugarcane fields north of town.

Watching filthy beggars struggle through abandoned stacks of crates, searching for anything valuable enough amidst the rotten remains of discarded vegetables, reminded Drake of his duties, lest he was going to suffer the same fate.

He closed the shutters, easing the tired wench's slumber. Then, he reached out for his discarded clothes that lay in a chaotic display on the floor, like jetsam carried by the morning's tide. The faded brown leather breeches, he already wore, having slept with them on, apparently. He single-handedly fastened the crotch's strings, at the same time employing his English smallsword to lift the dirty, white cotton shirt from the timbered floor, scaring a hiding mouse in the process. Passing the garment over his head, while still holding the blade with the right hand, he secured it at the waist with the bead-embellished, heavy-buckled belt he never parted with—a memento of his exploits in the Spanish Main.

Last, he slipped on the tall leather boots, fastening them at the back of the calf. They were poor affairs, ill-tended and cracked at the seams, a shadow of their past glory—just like Drake himself.

Someone knocked at the door.

"Damn you to hell and be gone," he said while struggling with the left boot.

"Captain Davies," a burly voice seeped through the door. "You're expected at Admiralty. At once."

He smirked. Partying had been wise, last night. For this was the day of apologies and sorrow.

And he had a bad feeling about it.

****

Admiral Red Leg was waiting for him.

"Drake! You old scoundrel, I was eager for your return," exclaimed Red Leg at the sight of the young captain entering his office. "That's good news to me."

Morgan 'Red Leg' O'Neill, nicknamed the 'Admiral' because he was one of the most influential men in Port Royal, was the only survivor of Captain Henry Morgan's failed assault to Puerto Principe in Cuba. Henry Morgan was destined to become the greatest member of the Brethren of the Coast had they not been slain in that perfectly planned attack-turned-into-a-trap. When he showed up in Port Royal claiming the Dons were ready to attack Jamaica, Red Leg was hailed as a hero. Thanks to this information, the raid was successfully repealed and he was commissioned by Governor Thomas Modyford as Captain of the Colonial Militia. For an Irish slave, sent to the colonies by Cromwell, it had been a great personal victory to gain such position among the Englishmen. Born in Ireland, before the Plague, Morgan O'Neill was of noble heritage. Yet, he lost all his privileges when Oliver Cromwell subdued the Irish Revolt of 1649. Morgan became a footpad at first, just to survive, then joined a band of brigands to prey on Puritans and finance Royalists' coffers. An idealist, Morgan embraced his Catholic upbringing, preferring an Anglican king rather than a Puritan tyrant. For years, he fought against Parliamentarians as a highwayman, until Charles II was restored to the throne. Yet, things did not go as he'd expected. Most of the land that Royalist supporters had lost in England was returned to them. This didn't happen in Ireland, however, and the old aristocracy was outraged. They had fought Parliamentary forces for the king, so why shouldn't they get their lands back? They formed themselves into bands called *Rapparees* and began raiding Protestant settlements, robbing from the rich and giving to the poor, finally united with their lower-class Catholic neighbors. These brave rogues lived in the hills of Wicklow, Tipperary, and other remote areas, swooping down at night and staying hidden by day. Betrayed by his king, Morgan became infamous as the *Red Fox*, a *rapparee* operating near Tipperary, until he was apprehended and sent to Barbados as a slave. There, he became one of the colony's '*Red Legs*', so named because of their easily sunburned fair-skin. Forced to work in a sugar plantation for the Speight Company of Bristol, he led a slave-revolt, captured a merchant ship, and turned to piracy. With his crew of former slaves, Captain Red Leg preyed on Spanish, French, and English ships alike, until he opted for pardon at Port Royal and became a privateer. After the Chaos Years, during which all support was lost from the homeland, Jamaica fell into turmoil and civil war, as different groups battled for supremacy in that tiny colony. At last, the League of the Antilles won by might of arms, supported by merchant's gold and piratical interests, and Modyford's royalists were hung at every lamppost. Modyford himself was lynched by the hungry mobs.

They had behaved no different from the Risen.

"Look, Morgan, I had a problem with the straggler—" Drake started apologizing, but was immediately shushed by Red Leg.

"Belay it! I don't care if you returned so early and without a prize on the tail. It's fairly evident that you botched it. Anyway, me dear friend, I've got something higher into me mind, than gold."

Drake stared at him, and then glanced back at the two heavily armed, evil-looking men standing guard. Better to look for a quick way out just in case this *higher thing* had something to do with his neck and a rope.

Red Leg's office was large, and exquisitely fitted with a sturdy, but finely, carved table covered by charts. Behind the table stood a plush chair, on which Morgan sat clutching a glass filled with red wine. A rarity these days; clearly a show of his influence. Not even the King of *Nouvelle France* in America could afford a single sip.

Drake gazed into Morgan's glowering icy-blue eyes, which were set in an oval face with a strong nose and a snow-white long mane. "What's this? A raid at St. Augustine? Or do you want to twist the Lion's tail at Jamestown?

Red Leg's laughter boomed in the large room. "Nay. None of that. We aren't talking lowly coups or sabotage of the Alliance war effort." He rose from his seat and, with a long stride, came closer to the younger captain. "This is an errand of mercy."

What was he talking of? Mercy and Red Leg were as opposite as cats and dogs. This old man had sent to the Almighty more than one-hundred souls.

"A little bird told me you were planning to leave for Tortuga."

"Nay, Morgan. I won't be here enjoying your company and," he pointed to the lonely glass of wine on the desk, "your good manners, if me planned that."

Red Leg glanced back at the crystal glass, then returned his gaze to him, lifting an eyebrow. "Oh, you want that? I do sincerely apologize for my lack of courtesy, Captain." He bowed ceremoniously, then snapped his fingers.

Immediately, the two goons were on Daniel, seizing his arms.

"Do you think you deserve that, old scoundrel?" Morgan wasn't really upset; he was playing with him. Drake spotted the light of amusement in his icy eyes. "Why did you moor your vessel at *Northdocks*, instead of the usual *Turtle Crawles*? I know you're fond of the *Crawles*, Drake. Unless…"

"I know what you're thinking, Morgan, but isn't like that. Told you, I wouldn't be here. I had my opportunity at Tortuga a couple days ago." He smiled at one of the goons. "Now tell this ape of yours to take his dirty hands off me, would you?"

"Tell me why you docked there first."

Drake grinned. "Had to show an old friend I was alive and kicking. You know about me rivalry with Le Boussier. He was sure I wasn't coming back from this raid in Donnish waters."

"Indeed." Red Leg returned to his desk and took the glass of wine. "Speaking of old friends. I met another friend of yours here last day. Master Silas Kater, the Dutch, said I should say, 'hello' should I run into you."

Drake didn't flinch. "He did? Very nice of him."

Morgan O'Neill motioned for the thugs to push the young captain forward. "Aye, very nice, considering the large sum of money I hear you owe him." He had him sniff the wine. Nothing else.

"Morgan, I see your men don't see a *chica* by ages, but please, tell this one on me left to stop holding me so tight."

Red Leg smirked. "That wit. That wit of yours is gonna cost your head, y'know?" Then he snapped his fingers again, and the two brutes let him go.

Immediately, and without turning, Drake kicked back like a wild stallion planting the heel of his right boot straight into the groin of one of goons. The large man yelped like a wounded dog, reached for his genitals, then fell down like a sack full of potatoes. The other swung a roundhouse at him, but Daniel easily dodged it and quickly jabbed him square into the jaw, then sunk his right fist into the large man's belly, causing air to escape off him like a blowpipe.

"Enough!" Red Leg shouted. Drake heard the click of the flintlock long before the cold metal touched the back of his neck. "We have business to discuss. Stop messing with the kids."

Both guards stared at him with eyes full of rage, but Drake knew they wouldn't disobey an order from their boss.

"Fine to me." Drake turned and defiantly removed the glass from the Admiral's fingers, "Thanks for offering." He gulped down the wine in one swig.

Red Leg smiled and shook his head. "You never change, don't you?" He turned to his men. "Learn from this man, boys. He is the contrary of everything I taught you."

"You taught 'em well," snapped Drake, cleaning the glass with his finger and licking the last drops out of it.

Morgan took off the glass from his hand and placed it back on the desk. "I want to introduce you to a special flower borne out these accursed islands. Follow me," he said, then signaled his enforcers to stand guard while he led Drake to a side door.

The pair entered a lavishly furnished bedroom, partly illuminated by bright candles, in which a comfortable bed, covered by a brocade bedspread lined in silver, dominated it as a dragon warding its hoard. In a darkened corner, a shadowy figure rose and came into view.

Drake's heart stopped for an instant at the sight, as she was the most beautiful creature he had ever seen.

Perfect features, highlighted by lovely cheeks, were encased into a chocolate-brown face, as smooth and healthy as to seem unreal. Her figure was wavy and dainty, clearly shown by her lace vest from which a full bosom caught the eye of the onlooker.

"Kaya, this is Captain Daniel Drake," said Red Leg, breaking the spell.

The girl lifted her hazelnut eyes to meet Daniel's, and he felt a shivering sensation run to his stomach. "So, dis da man who will bring we t' *Mabouyacay*?" She spoke with a typical Creole accent. One more point: Drake couldn't resist a lassie with a French lilt.

"Aye. He's the captain of the *Banshee's Cry*, the

fastest vessel on these waves. The perfect ship to carry out your master's will," replied Red Leg.

"*Le Baron* is no me *maître*," she said abruptly, coming closer to Drake, never lifting her stare from his eyes. "Me serve da *Loa*'s will, yet none is me mastah."

He couldn't spill out a single word, too charmed by the girl's beauty, or something else. '*What's happening to me?*' he thought.

Kaya came face-to-face and stared deeply into his eyes, looking for something. Then, she returned her attention to Red Leg.

"*Oui*. Dis is da righ' man. We have a deal, O'Neill."

CHAPTER THREE

<u>*KAYA*</u>

Later, they sat around a round table, enjoying a supper of roasted chicken and vegetables. Red Leg had explained him that Kaya was a *Mambo*, a voodoo priestess who could communicate with powerful spirits called the *Loas*.

She was from Tortuga, born amidst the buccaneer villages. Somehow, French political and religious criminals and refugees had made into the Caribbean by the turn of the century. Hunted by the Spaniards as transgressors, they hid in the jungles of western Hispaniola and lived a primitive lifestyle in order to avoid detection and capture. There was little competition with the natives, for they had largely been exterminated by this time. In addition, all major Spanish settlements sat on the east coast. To survive, they began selling meat to the English and Dutch ships in the area; the Spaniards had been kind enough to introduce cattle, pigs, and horses during their first attempt at colonization, and the animals roamed wild, providing an excellent source of food. So, these wild French became known as buccaneers, after the method they used to smoke their meat. They had learned the technique from the last Arawak Indians, and it consisted in slowly cooking the meat on a grill of green wood, called a '*buccan*'. This smoked meat became very attractive to the non-Spanish traders of the isles, used to fish and vegetables. However, this led the Spaniards to hunt the buccaneers down, as they were selling food to the enemies of Spain. Such proved to be a big mistake.

The buccaneers began to retaliate. Using dugout canoes, they took small Spanish fishing boats as prizes; these in turn were used to capture larger vessels. Eventually, they had full-sized ships and began to raid Spanish shipping in earnest. By 1630, they had captured the island of Tortuga and started using it as a base. By 1640, they had long ceased to make jerky—piracy was becoming big business. Their ranks were swollen by English, Dutch, and African slaves, and even Caribs.

Tortuga was a small island off Hispaniola. The Spanish claimed it, of course—they claimed all lands in the New World—but never occupied it. After they began to persecute the buccaneers in Hispaniola, Tortuga was used as a buccaneer base and was colonized by the French government. With a rocky terrain and a good, easily defensible harbor, it also hosted a population of Arawak and Carib survivors. These Indians mixed their belief system with that of the African people, as many of the priests of the old African gods had been chained and sold as slaves in the New World and some had escaped to make their way to Tortuga. This gave birth to the Voodoo faith.

Voodoo was a study of the spirit, both within and without the flesh, and like many primal faiths, it sought to explain the origins of the soul. Voodoo practitioners worshiped the *Loa* and revered the dead. These *Loa* were powerful spiritual beings, gods, and archetypes of human experiences that had enough connection to the material world to still understand and sympathize with humanity. Voodoo held all humans had two different energies within them that, along with the flesh, summed up their being: the *gros-bon-ange* or 'soul' and the *petit-bon-ange* or 'spirit'. The *gros-bon-ange* was a perfect spiritual copy of the individual from which it came, the totality of one's experiences, abilities and intelligence, but it had no concept of morality. That belonged to the *petit-bon-ange*, which was the seat of the conscience.

"So please, Kaya, let Drake be partaken of the true story of the Plague," Red Leg appealed.

The sky had darkened over Port Royal, foreboding a storm.

The Creole girl clutched her silver medallion, bearing the etched image of a coiled snake, and then began her story.

"Dis tale has been tole t' me by *le Baron Samedi*

'imself, during one ceremonial mounting." She released hold of the medallion. It sunk in her ample bosom. "In da year 1663, Commodore Hackett convinced jur King to approve an expedition t' *Las Tortugas*. Dem isles, now known as Cayman—according t' da will of jur namesake's hero, Captain Drake—were first visited by Christopher Columbus in 1503. Hackett had found a secret log of da Italian explorer in which 'im recounted of unholy ceremonies performed by natives—named *Kalinago*—into a cave complex called *Mabouya's Well*."

A lightning appeared on the horizon and the wind increased in strength. Indeed, a storm was coming.

"Hackett, being a fervent Christian, saw in it da Pit of da Devil and dem natives as debauched Satan-worshipers. 'Im reported to King Charles dat Cayman Brac hid a secret Spanish fortress dat could have been a threat to Jamaica's fledging colony. Believing t' commodore, jur King allowed ten warships, under Hackett's command, t' set sail t' *Mabouyacay*—as natives called da isle—and once dere, 'im put all inhabitants t' sword, set villages t' fire, and finally killed da shamans of dem cave."

She paused, gulping a glass of water, eyeing Drake's skeptic look. Drops of rain started to play on the porch's tiles while the black girl continued her tale.

"What Hackett no did know, was dese *Kalinago*

were *buyeis*, shamans whose role was t' perform rituals t' keep *Mabouya* at bay."

"Who's this *Mabouya*?" Drake inquired. The rain was increasing its rhythm, now quickly turning into a downpour.

"A spirit, *mon capitaine*, a demon of death and decay. Its purpose is t' taint dis world. Infect it with its essence, subverting da balance. Mastah of disease, taint, and decomposition, *Mabouya* exists only t' spread chaos. Yet, its disease is no goal, but a means. It frees its pestilence so dat everything can be infected by itself, as its final goal is omnipresence. It no craves total destruction or dominance, but it want to be part of everything, introducing its being in all living things. Released from its prison, da *djab* changed da very island of *Mabouyacay*. A fetid bog, swarming with disgusting things, replaced da sandy beaches, and da ocean's salty breeze was changed with da stench of evil. Dem dry cliffs became clammy and crumbly, home of festering rats and poisonous snakes. Da sky ovah da island is always covered by dark clouds, showering da cay with a viscid rain. When it's no raining da air itself looks make out of thick green powdha. Everywhere is a mix of life and death, as decomposing carcasses spawn more monstrosity."

Drake turned his face toward Red Leg, lifted an eyebrow showing his scorn, and rose from his seat. "I think I'm wasting me precious time, Morgan. Now, if you excuse me, I have to look for a potential customer for me next errand. As you know, ships do not sail by themselves and—"

"Belay it and sit down, Drake!" O'Neill's eyes were burning.

"No, you lissen, Red Leg. You turned me into a *lapdog* with those accursed letters of Marque, when all I wanted was freedom and to be my own master. I signed the League's statement just because I was given no choice. But you can't force me to stay here, listening to fairytales—"

Red Leg produced his flintlock and squared it at him. "I said sit down, Daniel. I find your lack of faith amusing, but your disrespect offensive. I don't know why I allowed you so much free reign till now."

"Because you find me cute? Maybe?" Drake kept his roguish smile, but returned to his chair. There was rage in the Admiral's eyes and something else … something new that scared the hell out of him.

"*Lapdog.*" Red leg put away the pistol. "You still use that derogatory term for privateers. After all these years, I thought I had made a genteel person out of you. But you are still pirate scum."

Kaya had been silent, impassibly watching the exchange. But now her gaze was on him. For as beautiful as she was, Drake couldn't shake off a feeling of uneasiness. She was like a snake mesmerizing a mouse. And *he* was the mouse.

"Kaya, my dear," said Red Leg, patting her hand, "please go on with your story. I will ensure meself Captain Drake will not interrupt you again."

Kaya smiled and nodded. Then went on. "With no one t' make sacrify, da evil spirit enraged and sent da Plague into dis world. The sailors of Hackett's fleet became embodiment of da Curse and when dem returned to England dem carried it with dem."

Drake looked into Red Leg's eyes. The man believed this nonsensical stuff.

"Da *Loa* are no happy with da current state of affairz," continued Kaya, "especially *Baron Samedi*, for 'im is judge of da dead. He tole me how t' lift da *Curse of Mabouya* and me know how t' pass into Risen's water without harm."

Red Leg's face eased into a smile. "It is now clear what the *Banshee*'s role will be? We'll be heroes, Drake. We'll be saviors for lifting this curse from humankind!"

"You're crazy!" Drake blew off. "Blimey! Do you eat it?" He wasn't going to lead his men into Risen territory to be slaughtered.

"I'm not crazy, Drake. I'm a believer." Red Leg rebuked, showing his own silver medallion, then, added, "And you're coming with me Drake, because you know what I'll do, should you refuse."

He paused to get Drake's full attention, because he was now staring at the woman's bosom.

"I'll have your crew jerk in the Devil's arms for treason. You know you still owe Kater the Dutch six damned missed payments, and by League's law I can sentence you and all your scurvy dogs to be hung till death comes."

Drake's eyes widened. Morgan could do that, he knew the old bastard had the power.

He took a deep intake, then, ignoring the older man, asked the *Mambo*, "Assuming I accept to lead me lads to certain doom, how you think we can stop a *god*?"

"Dere is no god ovah dere," she replied, grinning. "Just an evil spirit: a being we call a *djab*. No one knows how dis djab was trapped into da pit, or by who, but it's free and da only way t' return it t' imprisonment is t' perform a *caille* ceremony at da well—a sacrify."

"And this should be enough to stop the *Curse*?"

"Me was raised t' be a Mambo, Captain Drake, and me know how t' perform. Da rite was taught t' me mothah by *Ghedé*, da Lord of da Dead."

"But how you think a single ship can intrude into the fiend's territory? We'll be diced to the last!" Drake spat at O'Neill.

"There's a way," stated Red Leg in a gravelly voice.

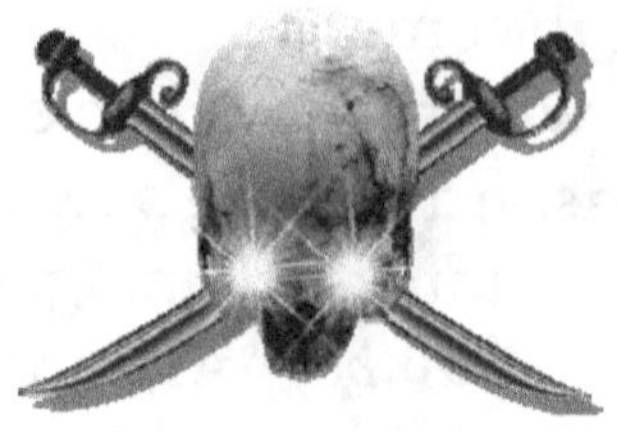

CHAPTER FOUR

THE FRENCHMAN

"You can't take the sea from me, Red Leg...," Drake uttered while keeping an eye on the two thugs that were blatantly following him in the twisted alleys of the Warehouse district. The Admiral wanted to be sure he and his crew weren't about to jump for the Blue. Usually, Daniel wouldn't even think about it, for doing so would brand you as a traitor of the Brethren, and no port would be safe for your boat to dock at.

But this time was different.

The Admiral had gone crazy. He believed in all that voodoo crap. Fine for him, let him get skinned alive by the Risen for nothing. But not his crew. He was responsible for his men and his ship.

Because here, in the Caribbean Sea, a crew was the closest thing to a family. You've got yourself a ship and a crew; you cared for them. You brought them into danger, but you had to offer them a goal, a prize. Most of them didn't consider you family and would happily slice your throat for one doubloon more, but you, as their captain, had to care for them.

And you cared for the ship, too, for she was your home, your workplace, and your lover. To take care of her you had to man her with the best, keep her keel clean, and repair the damage she suffered out there. All that care needed money. And you needed a job. When your boat was out in the Blue, there were just as many ways to earn pesos as there were to get riddled with holes. Trick was to do more of the former and less of the latter. Some jobs were simple: hauling passengers, shipping cargo—some legitimate, some not so much. Others were more complex: dodge Alliance and Donnish patrols, avoid being caught by jackals of the sea—those damned souls who had chosen a nomadic life to stay away from all laws and regulations—and pray the Risen never got a sniff of you.

To save his crew from certain doom, he had to find money soon to repay the Dutch all his debt, so taking off the only card Red Leg could play against him.

Yet, Drake's day did not improve. He spent the rest of the morning at the docks, working his contacts to no avail. He was up for any scheme that would net him some money quickly, but the only opportunity he found was to sign on to another privateer as a crewman. Daniel had done his years as lowly swab, and he would not go back to such abuse. He was a captain, dammit, and he was not about to let some other buccaneer order him around. More, he had no time.

By afternoon, he was tired, and with the tropical storm drenching Port Royal, he decided to return to the *Black Gull* and talk to Mac. Maybe he had found something with his innumerable contacts. He worked his way through the streets of Scurvytown, weaving through the crowds of hawkers, workers, thieves, and hookers. Garishly clothed hucksters tried to hustle him into gambling houses and partner him with rough-looking women, but Drake brushed them all off. No time for games and lust. Besides, now that he thought of it … he felt none.

He kept thinking about the black woman. Yes, she was crazy, still…

He was nearing the tavern's door, dowsed and sullen, when a hand grabbed his shoulder and spun him around. "Are you Daniel 'Drake' Davies?" asked a voice with a French accent.

Drake looked at the intruder. He was an elegant foppish lad, clad in exquisite clothes with a rapier and main gauche hanging from his gilded belt, and a broad-brimmed hat sporting a pheasant plume. His fine features, and his cleanliness, made him stand out in Scurvytown like a peacock amidst chickens.

Maybe Lady Fortune had not abandoned him: this fop was wealthy, so he could be a potential patron. A higher-up looking for discreet passage into Alliance's waters?

"Yes, sir, I am Captain Drake, at your service," he replied. "How can I help you?"

The Frenchman's features clouded abruptly worse than the sky above Port Royal, just like he had, somehow, offended him. Then, unexpectedly, the foreigner drew both blades out. "You can help me ... by dying, pirate!"

Quickly, Daniel unsheathed his smallsword. '*Now what?*' he thought, then uttered a curse to Lady Luck, getting ready to defend from this lunatic. "Did I meet you before? You don't look so familiar."

The Frenchman didn't answer, he just thrust forward with the rapier, but Drake easily parried the strike with a downward swing of his own blade. "Weird," he continued, "Most of those who want to kill me have at least crossed me path before. Yet..."

In a flash, the Frenchman vaulted across the distance between them, attempting a swift kick at Drake's hand, trying to disarm him.

"Nice move, lad," Drake spat while dodging the kick and jumping sideways. "But please, let me finish me line before attacking. Let's try to be genteel. First, lemme know the name of who I am about to send to the Almighty."

The young man circled around him, looking for a weak spot in Drake's defense. "I'm Claude Armand Mont Blanc, musketeer of His Royal Highness King Louis of *Nouvelle France*, scum!"

Drake shrugged. "Never heard of you."

"I have come to this wretched city on a quest for the captain of the pirate ship *Banshee's Cry*."

"That's me ship," said Drake, as he tested the musketeer's defenses with a quick thrust. The boy did not flinch at the attack and deftly swept the smallsword aside. Drake stepped back as the lad's main gauche stabbed for his gut. It seemed the Frenchman was skilled.

Claude flicked his rapier at Drake's eyes, but he ducked and stepped back, then used his left hand to pull out his dagger. He preferred fighting with just his sword, but facing two weapons, he decided to even the odds.

By now, a crowd began to gather. A fight in Scurvytown was not remarkable, but one involving a wealthy foreigner was most unusual. Nor was this some barroom brawl but a real duel between two skilled swordsmen. It didn't take long for the gamblers in the crowd to start taking bets.

"It seems we have some company," said Drake, grinning at the crowd. "Now that you have an audience, perhaps you'd like to tell me why you're trying to kill me."

The musketeer charged with his rapier high and main gauche low. Daniel parried with both his own weapons, and the blades locked together. Now that they were up close, he could see the hatred in the boy's eyes.

"Six months ago your ship attacked and sank a ship from *Nouvelle Orleans* named *Le Guisarme*," said Mont Blanc through gritted teeth. "For this act of piracy, you will pay with your life."

The two combatants pushed and strained, each looking to free a blade and plunge it home. "Piracy me *huevos*," spat Drake. "We were a privateer ship with a Letter of Marque in good order."

"We both know that *privateer* is just a polite word for a pirate, you scum," replied Mont Blanc. "The Kingdom of *Nouvelle France* won't have it."

Drake pushed the man off, and both fighters fell back into fencing stances. The crowd howled for blood now that the blades were free. "*Nouvelle France* won't have it, or *you* won't?" he asked. "Your king knows the rules. Hell, he's hired League's privateers more than once. I've killed Dons under your flag!"

The thought of Drake fighting for his king was too much for Mont Blanc to bear. He came on fast, cutting and thrusting with his rapier while his main gauche probed for an opening. Drake gave ground and parried desperately. He stopped the worst of the attacks but lost track of the main gauche during the final flurry of blows. He realized his error too late and could not evade the small blade.

"My brother was the captain of *Le Guisarme*," growled Mont Blanc as he drove the main gauche deep into Drake's shoulder, "and I will avenge him."

In retort, Drake kicked the lad in the shin, throwing the musketeer off balance enough for him to back away. His shoulder was on fire, and he knew he needed to finish this fight before the blood loss finished it for him. He let his dagger clatter to the pavement. With the blood running down his arm, the hilt was too slick to hold anyway.

"I remember your brother," Daniel said casually as he slowly stepped backwards, left hand probing behind him. In a few paces, he backed into a building. He smiled as his fingers dug into the shoddy concrete typical of Scurvytown construction. He locked eyes with Mont Blanc. "Yes, that brother of yours was quite the bold captain. He sent his men to certain death, then he begged for mercy like a courtesan. He died a coward's death."

"Liar!" the musketeer screamed and charged Drake anew. The Frenchman's face was warped by rage as he thrust his rapier at the pirate's heart. Drake deflected the blow to the side and then used his left hand to fling concrete dust into Mont Blanc's eyes. The coarse flecks of stone blinded him.

Drake sidestepped his opponent's wavering blade and drove his sword through the lad's guts. As Drake pulled his blade free, Mont Blanc crumpled to the wet ground, and the crowd roared its approval.

"You should have stayed in *Nouvelle France*," spat Drake. "Now your mother has lost two sons."

"That was a dirty trick," the young man gasped.

"You have no honor, pirate filth."

Drake laughed. "You Alliance blades are always prattling on about honor. Maybe that means something over there, but this is Port Royal. Here we fight to win."

"May God curse this wretched city!"

"What makes you think he hasn't?" said Drake, but Mon Blanc never heard the retort.

Claude Armand Mont Blanc, musketeer of *Nouvelle France*, was already dead.

****

The wound in his shoulder throbbed, but Daniel Drake was smiling.

The money in the Frenchman's purse was more than enough to pay back the Dutch. Now all he had to do was sell the musketeer's rapier, and he'd be able pay his crew. He hated to part with the blade, as it was exquisitely crafted, but he had to. After taking care of his wounded shoulder, Drake lay on his cot to get some rest. His long day was over.

Yet, his night had just begun.

CHAPTER FIVE

DEAD IN THE WATER

Drake kept turning in his bed.

The unexpected duel with the Frenchman should have tired him beyond belief, yet he could not fall to slumber. Something was amiss.

His mind kept going to Kaya.

There was something magnetic in that girl, something he had never experienced before. He felt attracted to her in an unnatural way. And this scared him.

Drake had had his share of pretty company, and had fallen in love once with a Frenchwoman he had held for ransom after capturing her ship. The plan had been to kidnap the bride-to-be of the Governor of _Provence Louisienne_, but it turned out the lass was just her maid, a decoy organized by the French to ensure safe transport of the Governor's _belle_. They had targeted the wrong ship, and wasted time at chasing and boarding the lure ship while the real freighter traveled on a safer route. The League's agents had fallen for the French ruse and fed Drake false information.

Worthless, the servant was destined to become yet another addition to the growing prostitute population of Port Royal or Tortuga, but Drake became fond of her. A pretty little thing, the young woman was possessed by a combative spirit. Nonetheless, she used her guile and charm to get the captain's protection, but once in Port Royal she disappeared quickly, leaving him with a broken heart, short of ten doubloons, and a bitter attitude toward love.

However, what he felt for Kaya wasn't love, but lust. He couldn't stop thinking about her sinuous body, the way she moved like a wildcat, the curve of her full lips…

Outside, the tropical storm had calmed down, leaving the city wet. Drake went at the window and opened it to enjoy the cool aroma and listen to drips of escaping trapped water on gambrel roofs. He noticed a dense fog was coming westerly, approaching fast, and looking like an enormous wave of titanic proportions.

The smell of drenched plants and sweet tang of sugarcane reached his nose, and he surprised himself thinking again of Kaya. He imagined her ebony body entwining with his own, her long legs closing behind his thrust.

And he decided to pay her a nightly visit.

****

A thick fog blanketed the entire harbor and

seeped through Port Royal like a river of ghosts. Yet, above Fort Charles, high on the bluff, the sky was clear, and a full moon shone, casting an eerie glow on the seaport.

Out on the sea, barely visible, deep in the twirling thick fog, something moved toward the bay, something with blackened and tattered sails that fluttered under absent winds. Like a great white shark's dorsal fin silently slicing though the water, its mainmast pierced the mists.

For a ship out of Hell had come to Port Royal.

****

Boys as young as seven or eight were often welcome aboard as crew because they were cheap, yet ten to twelve was the more common starting age. They served as personal servants to the ship's officers, and performed menial tasks.

On warships, small boys known as *powder monkeys* carried fresh loads to the gun crews, and marine snipers on enemy ships did their best to kill them.

Unlike in the Alliance, where kids were schooled and protected as they were the fighters of tomorrow's wars, the League's society still clung to pre-plague ideals and did not value children, who were expected to work as soon as they were physically able. More, cabin boys were sexually exploited by some captains, and the crew scorned such unfortunate children, calling them *bum boys.*

The Caribbean Sea was not a happy place to be a child.

While they retained the need to play, such was not seen as a child's province, and they were often beaten for neglecting a duty or when surprised playing with something that wasn't theirs.

Willie Kurt was one of such kids. Despised by the *Roosendaal*'s crew for being the captain's relief, he was humiliated and mistreated by anyone aboard the Dutch vessel. Eight years old, thin and frail, Willie had decided enough was enough. So, when the trader had docked in Port Royal, he had made a knapsack out of his ragged shirt, filled it with stale bread and a moldy slice of *Gouda* cheese, then slithered out of the freighter as an eel out of a fishing net.

He was now frolicking along the *Turtle Crawles*, barefooted, hopping from barrel to barrel in a game of his own fantasy: the space between casks was the dangerous open sea—home of Davey Jones—and the containers themselves were like a treacherous pathway made of islets and rocky shoals. To fall would mean his death.

Willie sang an English rhyme while jumping, punctuating it with yells of '*yay!*' everytime he succeeded in the vaulting.

"Bloody Bones, Bloody Bones,
What do you see?
I see people full of vanity."
The fog was now cloaking the docks and Willie

felt a chillness seeping into his bones. A lonely stray dog, which was looking for scraps amidst the garbage, suddenly lifted its head and started to bark in direction of the harbor, causing Willie to lose his balance and land on the rotten planks.

"Belay it, ye stinky licebag!"

The dog ignored him and kept baying. Enraged, the kid snatched up a piece of wood and threw it at the beast. "Be gone!"

The animal easily dodged the impromptu projectile, circled around, then came closer to the fetid dock waters, but it sniffed something was wrong, yelped, and ran away with the tail between its legs.

"Stupid mutt," grumbled Willie, and then climbed again on one of the tallest barrels.

From that height, he noticed the dockyard cats were bolting away, screeching and hissing, disturbed by an unknown source of fear. Willie thought sharks were feasting in the pier's dark water as more than one ship had discarded the putrid content of the galleys at sunset.

"Bloody Bones, Bloody Bones
Where do you hide?
In pools and mirrors, full of pride."

He flipped gaily from the tall container to a shorter one. "Yay!"

Meanwhile, the fog had turned so dense he could barely see his next objective. So, he decided to cheat; after all, it was a solitary game and no grownup was around to lecture him on the principles of always sticking by the rules. He jumped down the cask and padded along an empty mooring, down to the end of it. "Victory!" In his eight-year-old mind, full of daring heroes and distressed damsels, he had just reached his final port.

Bubbles frothed in the brackish waters.

The kid bent over, trying to get a closer look at whatever was causing the commotion. Nervous, he kept singing his rhyme.

"Bloody Bones, Bloody Bones,
Will you come for me?"

Yet, he didn't finish it, as the grinning, yellow-skinned unliving thing, which was lurking underwater, reached up and dragged the frightened boy down.

"Look in the water and wait and see," said the fiend, then drowned young Willie Kurt.

****

In her quarters at Red Leg's mansion, Kaya watched as pea-soup fog replaced the storm that had been hitting Port Royal by morning. The *Loa* were restless.

She closed the heavy French doors and returned to the pentagram she had previously drawn. All the candles surrounding it were now dead. Carefully, she replaced them with new ones, and lit them one after another, until all came to life.

Then she stepped inside the pentagram, and removed the black felt cloth from the small object at its center. The flickering light sparked on the clear surface of a minute crystal skull with black onyx eyes.

She couldn't shake off the sensation of unease as she began her chanting. Even after all these years, even after all her teachings, she was still afraid of the *Loa*. Her mother had told her not to be afraid of them, for her heart was pure, that fear was the province of the *duppies*—the *Loa* mockers—and the duppies were attracted to it like moths to a flame.

According to Voodoo, *duppies* were evil spirits, found in everyone but stronger in some people more than others. Specifically, voodooists believed that a *duppy* was released from particularly evil individuals who died violent deaths during storms. This spirit was usually unable to act with any great power, merely causing mischief and minor ill fortune to its enemies, but with the onset of a storm, it began to grow in power.

So, mass devastation wasn't the only horror powerful storms brought with them. That was also the time when *duppies* came out.

Destroying a *duppy* wasn't easy, but many Mambos in Hispaniola possessed the spells required to exorcise such a demon. Their spells pitted the caster's will directly against the power of the *duppy*. However, before doing so, the

Mambo had to learn the identity of the *duppy*, and this could take weeks or it could even be impossible.

Kaya knew a *duppy* had followed her here in Port Royal. And she had to face it.

The ritual to identify the *duppy* involved a great deal of chanting and dancing, where Kaya had to wait for one of the *Loa* to mount her. Once the *Loa* was in residence, she would ask it the name of the spirit. If appeased, the *Loa* would name it and Kaya could create the proper powders and spells to ensure it was banished forever from this realm.

But her ritual was interrupted by a crash as the French doors' glass shattered and the wood splintered under the strength of a yet-unseen force.

Calmly, Kaya stood, ready to face the intruders, and discovered she had it wrong.

The *duppy* wasn't the only horror that had followed her in Port Royal.

****

A noose dangled in the courtyard gallows waiting for the neck of tomorrow's condemned.

Two League guards were prattling about what was the most powerful ship in the Caribbean: the *Raven's Nest* or the *Banshee's Cry*. The first one, a paunchy individual with a bulbous nose going by the name of Farnsworth, asserted that while the

Raven's Nest was certainly better equipped to deal with enemy fire, the *Banshee* had no ship who could match her speed. The second, a tall man, extremely thin and with long limbs, named Cartwright, disputed his companion's claims by the fact that speed alone was worthless when faced by the powerful spring-loaded culverins of the Alliance's Peacekeepers.

"I agree on that, Cartwright. Yet, you must concede there are better ships out there than those two paragons of the sea," said Farnsworth, stopping at the parapet to look down at the gibbet. Ernst the Jew would occupy that empty noose tomorrow morning, ending a life of treachery, scams, and viciousness.

Cartwright leaned on the side. "For example?"

"The *Scarlet Witch*!"

Farnsworth scoffed. "That's a legend! That ship doesn't count!"

"Yes, it does," insisted Cartwright.

"We're talking about real ships, matey, not ones out of tavern tales."

"The *Scarlet Witch* does exist," rebuked Cartwright, red in the face. "Gorman the Red has seen it by his own deadlights."

Slowly, the fog was engulfing the whole fort, hiding the sea and the docks from their sight. Farnsworth instinctively shivered as the vapors wetted his uniform's cloth. Even weirder was the ill air current—not a true wind, for it had no certain direction—that banged the wood and metal fittings on ships' lines against the vessel masts, and spun the weather vanes on the town's roofs, each one on a casual direction.

"So, you believe that a ghost ship, crewed by devils and..." Farnsworth couldn't finish his ironic comment because a loud boom thundered in the harbor, soon followed by a whistling sound.

"Cannons!" shouted Cartwright.

Then the parapet wall exploded and both men were swept away by a large ball of fiery metal.

****

The fog lit up at every shot of the mysterious ship's cannons. Sitting at the center of the harbor, she targeted both the fort and the town. Out of the mists, round projectiles brought a more lethal rain on Port Royal, as the broadsides released by the hidden vessel battered the streets and alleys on the dockside, shattering moored ships and buildings alike. Those unlucky villagers who were out for the night panicked and scattered away randomly, looking for shelter, as debris flew everywhere and the stinging smoke of spent gunpowder mixed with the already dense vapors of the fog. Soon, fires started to appear and the warning bells of the colony's forts began to ring desperately. Chaos ensued as members of the militia swarmed to the docks to face this unforeseen threat. Port Royal had never been attacked before—except for the failed Donnish raid before the Plague, but that had been largely a naval battle fought closer to Manatee Bay than in the inner harbor—as the League capital was one of the most defended cities in the Caribbean. Trying to attack such a garrisoned town was foolish and suicidal. Yet, someone had dared to bring havoc to Port Royal that night and was going to face the weight of such ill-advised deed, because soon all the guns of the ships in the harbor, and the cannon batteries on Fort Charles and Fort James, would be trained at the flashes in the mist. The League soldiers and mariners couldn't see the enemy in the water; nonetheless, the night's air was filled with the sound of blasting artillery as every bronze in the port chanced for their mark.

And whatever was in the mists ceased its hammering of the town.

A moment later, an explosion echoed across the water and a giant sphere of flames brightened the fog, for an instant revealing the silhouette of a large galleon on fire.

Cheers replaced the sound of cannons as the proud defenders of Port Royal began to laugh and jump in frenzied celebration. Obviously, the attackers had a powder hold so filled up that volleys from the forts and the ships' combined fire had hit and ignited its content. As if to confirm this, a second rumbling detonation, so powerful that buildings on the shorefront trembled in resonance, silenced the revelers, soon followed by a third and a fourth. The intense heat caused the mists to part in the area where the dying vessel sat, and lookouts could clearly see the massive warship fall apart in a matter of seconds. The large masts crashed down, gigantic cannons flung into the air like a kid's toys, and the whole hull collapsed in on itself while being engulfed by flames.

The enemy was gone.

Literally—one minute it had been there, consumed by the flames, then it had shattered in thousands of debris. Burning fragments, sails, and spars floated on the water surface, and soon the first bodies appeared. This prompted the first launch of longboats from the docks, the Leaguemen eager to know the attacker's identity.

Moonlight finally shone down the port's shallow waters, and its pale rays clarified wavering silhouettes in the shifting currents. Unseen by the cheering folk of Port Royal, the horde of shambling corpse-like creatures scuttled forward. Moving silently across the lagoon floor, the grinning dead marched toward the town's shore.

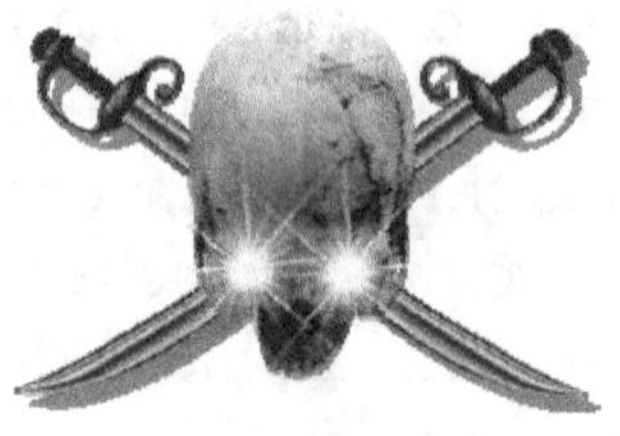

CHAPTER SIX

DEAD BY DAWN

Rising from the water and clambering on the docks, a relentless pack of withered, sword-wielding corpses swarmed to Port Royal. With discolored flesh, and swollen tongues protruding from blackened lips, they exuded a stench of dead flesh, polluted seawater, and massive decay. They had weapons grafted on their bodies, blades and flintlocks protruding like hellish extensions of their dead flesh. Some wore tattered red uniforms, their badges of rank long since faded away. Many had their eyes and mouths sewn shut, yet others had bulging and glossy eyes, like those of the hanged. All sported a hideous grimace on their face, as the lips and gums had receded showing their yellowish teeth. At their sight, the cheering ceased and looks of horror and despair smeared the faces of Port Royal's defenders, as they all knew the meaning behind the creatures' appearance.

The Plague had finally come to the New World.

****

Drake had almost reached Red Leg's mansion when he heard the sound of gunfire. It came from the harbor, soon followed by response shots from the forts, indicating a battle was in progress.

Who'd been so goosy to attack Port Royal? He was tempted to rush down to the docks, but the vision of the city militiamen's bluecoats darting amidst the alleys and pushing aside everyone on their path, had him change his mind. What if this was a decoy, a ruse to lure all able-bodied to battle at the harbor while infiltrators slithered in the city from inland? He had pointed that weakness in the city defense a dozen times to the Councilors, yet they had always refused to acknowledge the need for a garrison to be stationed northward, as they saw that as a waste of resources in the already dilapidated coffers of the League.

Somehow, his first thought ran to Kaya. He didn't know how, but he *knew* she was in danger. Something inside him screamed she had it right: there was indeed an evil spirit at *Mabouyacay* spreading madness and horror.

And Kaya knew how to stop it.

Shocked by his own resolve, Drake hastened to O'Neill's home.

****

Kaya prepared to face the intruders.

But the invaders that came crashing through the French doors weren't bloated Risen, or ghostly *duppies*. They looked filthy, ugly, with withered flesh and horrible grins. They were also pale beyond belief, and stank of the sea. All wore tattered red uniforms, but their insignia were long gone, and no medals decorated their chests. Their eyes were covered by a dull film, and the irises shone with a weird red light. Chuckling, the six leering maniacs spread around to cut any way out.

Kaya understood who these men were even before she heard the voice of their master.

"We see you've got something of ours, Miss."

Tall and imposing, sporting a bright red coat and long white hair, the man spoke in whispers. Under the shadow of a broad-brimmed hat sparkled two tiny dots of fire set inside pools of absolute darkness. Like his men, or even more, his face was gaunt and pale with a jolly grin; his skin tightly pulled on his frame and withered limbs. His left wrist ended in a stump with a vicious-looking reaping hook stained by dried blood.

"Me no agree, Crimson Roger," sputtered Kaya, her eyes locked on the cruel implant. "Me kan't see any of jurs here. Certainly no jur hand."

The Crimson Roger's eyes flashed, but he ignored her taunt, then signaled for his men to grab her. However, the ghastly thugs seemed to hesitate, tried to get closer, but stopped short of the pentagram's borders. "What's wrong with you, swabs?"

The ghoulish sailors looked at him, their leering faces a quiz for any mortal man, yet an open book for the Crimson Roger. His infernal eyes landed on the pentagram. "Oh, that. We see. Some old *magie noire*, we suppose."

"Ju are a long way from hommah, Captain," she snarled. "Me motha tole me t' watch out for ju."

The pirate turned his hideous face to her; the face of a grimacing skull. "Your mother, Miss? We're afraid your mother advised you wrong. Do you really think this—" he pointed at the arcane drawing, "—this pathetic trinket can hold cursed men at bay?" He made a step forward and cackled.

"*Oui*, me do believe so." She scooped the skull inside the black felt satchel.

"Miss Kaya," continued the Crimson Roger, "we can't see the point in this ... arguing. We don't want you, we just want the skull."

The sound of cannons could be heard in the distance, but the gaunt man seemed to ignore it.

"Nonetheless, we are gentlemen, and we won't allow the odious Risen to add you to their grisly collection. So, we will be more than glad to allow you safe passage aboard the *Scarlet Witch*."

"Me coming nowhere, and it will be bettah for ju t' call back jur servants—"

"How?" The Crimson Roger gestured toward the harbor. "Do you think we do command the Risen? Oh no, Miss, we may be far from home indeed, but you…" He placed one foot inside the pentagram. "You are far from the truth!" Suddenly, he reached out and grabbed Kaya by the neck, gaggling like a madman, "Nothing is as it seems. We aren't the terrible villains, the Risen do not serve us, and you, my dear Miss, aren't the powerful Mambo you believe to be."

Kaya struggled against the vise, trying to pry the cold, steely fingers open, but to no avail. He lifted her like a rag doll and pulled her toward his deathly grin. His cruel sickle pointed at her face. "As you can see, nothing is as it seems."

She noticed one of the ghastly crewmen had picked up a small clay lamp she used for her ceremonies. The creature held it by the ropes and stared at it, curious to know what was inside. And she smiled, causing befuddlement in the emaciated man. "Me know," she hissed, but the Crimson Roger couldn't hear her whisper, so he released his hold of the woman's throat, and grabbed instead her wrist. She was still clutching her satchel.

"You'd best hand it over to us or we'll retrieve it from your very dead hand." He looked down at the little bag.

"Me'll do, and on me own will," she said, gasping for breath. Her eyes ran again to the gangly sailor examining the voodoo lamp. The Crimson Roger noticed and, suspecting foul play, ordered his minion to bring him the item. Still training his hook at Kaya's throat, he released her wrist and palmed the spherical lamp.

"What's this? Why does it attract so much attention from you?" He was curious, his unquenchable thirst for knowledge showing. Maleah, Kaya's mother, had told her the Crimson Roger had been cursed by the Loa for both his wickedness and his curiosity. He had this weird habit of referring to himself in plural, like he was part of the whole crew. Maleah had explained that was due to the fact more than one soul inhabited his accursed body. She had also told her the Crimson Captain and his crew plied the seas in search of artifacts, and had a sixth sense for items of power. The red pirate was fascinated by the arcane because he was himself a *bokor*, an evil sorcerer.

"Ju said it." She moved fast and opened the small lid, instinctively closing her eyes. "No thing is as it seems."

The room was suddenly flooded by an explosion of white light and everything became smoky as the lamp released its mystical content.

"Do not allow her to flee!" the Crimson Roger bellowed. "Follow her, mindless idiots. Fetch the skull!"

****

Kaya was already running down the stairs when she noticed a figure storming inside the mansion from the front door. It was Drake. He spotted her.

"Kaya! Look out!"

A withered hand grabbed her shoulder and she acted blindly. Planting her elbow in the assailant's face, she broke his jaw. Then, she bolted down the stairs, but soon more hands grappled her ankles and arms. She tried to disengage, but when she felt her efforts were fruitless, she threw the small bag to Drake. "No let dem have it!"

Drake had drawn his smallsword, ready for combat; nonetheless, he snatched the satchel with his free hand, then rushed up to help her.

"Go!" Kaya yelled while one of the weird beings, cutlass raised high, came straight at him, wide-eyed and with a psychotic grin.

"No!" Drake thrust his blade forward with a flourish, catching the assailant in the chest. The man fell over and tumbled down the stairs. Five more burst through the door, soon followed by the man who led them.

"That's our treasure jangling in that purse, thief." A cruel sneer decorated the gaunt man's face as he placed the hook below Kaya's throat.

"Strange, *hermano*; I thought it belonged to the young lady."

The Crimson Roger laughed at the remark, and his men drew their sabers. "Kill him."

In a flash, Drake vaulted across the distance between them, launching a swift kick at Crimson's bladed hand. Then, he grabbed Kaya by her wrist and both rushed downstairs. But their path was barred by the same man Drake had just 'killed'. There was no blood on his body and no sign of the blade's deep wound. The grinning pirate swung his cutlass. Drake bounded onto the nearby table, easily parrying the maniac's weapon, while Kaya grabbed a tall iron chandelier and used it as a fighting pike, striking at the swarm of ghoulish thugs. She smashed it into the nearest brute's nose, hearing the satisfying crunch of bone. From the balcony, another creature hopped onto the table to face Drake. With a quick riposte, he slashed the man's sword-arm; the blade went flying and Daniel deftly caught it in his offhand. Another blow knocked the man off the table, sending him crashing into his compatriots with a thud.

"You gentlemen really should practice more." Drake raised the smallsword in a mock salute.

Another squad of monsters charged through the door. These had firearms implanted on their wrists. They leveled the guns at Drake and Kaya, clearly intending to kill them with a single volley.

"Do not kill the woman!" roared the Crimson Roger while he hurried downstairs.

Drake hurled his spare dagger in a rapid spinning motion, and the leering creatures easily dodged it. Yet, the weapon sliced neatly through a nearby rope, loosening the chandelier hanging above the great hall. He grasped the line with his free hand, holding Kaya at the waist with the other, as the wrought iron device came crashing down, allowing the momentum to pull them up to the second-floor balcony. Shots followed them all the way up, the bullets whistling a hair's breadth from Drake's chest. Kicking out his legs, he caught the balcony railing, then helped Kaya to regain her footing.

"Who's that guy? Never seen a talking Risen before," he asked, sheathing his sword, and diving into Kaya's room, all the way down to the crashed window.

"A cursahd man," answered Kaya. "Ignore 'im and bring me aboard jur ship."

"Ignore him? Are you joking? A cackling Risen?" But she wasn't; there was that stoic determination in her eyes that sent those darn shivers down Drake's spine.

Seagulls cried and the air hung damp with salt as they exited onto the balcony. From there, they climbed to the roof and raced to the edge. Just a short hop down the side and they'd be…

He skidded to a halt at the building's edge.

Below them, the estate walls dropped hundreds of feet before ending in the crashing tides. A few banners fluttered in the breeze below. "This won't be easy," he spat, then spun around at the hearing of footsteps, only to see the Crimson Roger and his men emerge from below, weapons drawn. They spread out along the rooftop, cutting off any hope of escape.

"There's nowhere to run, rapscallion." Crimson advanced slowly. "You're standing on the edge of Davey Jones' Locker."

"Then I'll send him your regards." Drake's face broke into a grim smile as he turned and he and Kaya leaped over the edge.

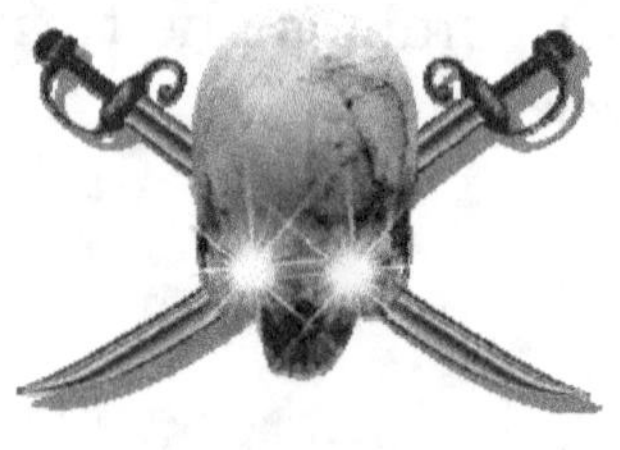

CHAPTER SEVEN

THE LAUGHING DEAD

Chaos reigned in Port Royal as the dead battled the living along the seafront. The undead swarmed from the water and the League Militias' bravest discharged their muskets uttering silent prayers to the Lord. Those who did not possess a daring—or foolish—soul became prey of panic and bolted in all directions, looking to keep distance from the bearers of the Plague. The walking dead attacked everyone, indiscriminately striking at the fighter and the villager, shooting their grafted flintlocks at every target that caught their attention, lopping off limbs and heads with their wicked blades, and setting fires.

Wendy Duquesne, a trollop and fixture of Port Royal's docks, was running for her own life, skidding on her precious brand new French shoes in the alleys, chased by two slavering monsters, when she bumped into Geist who was just coming out of *The Song of the Siren* tavern to look for what all that buzz was about. At the sight of him, an albino, she screamed, mistaking him for one of the attackers, then punched him right in the jaw and kept running.

Befuddled, Geist cursed her, and then turned his attention to the oncoming chasers. And his usual pallid skin turned even grayer, as he caught the nature of those beings. Without a second thought, he extracted his pistol and fired it at the closest one. Billowing smoke obscured his vision for an instant, and he could just hear the thump of something hitting the cobblestones, while bare feet splashed past him continuing their pursuance of the girl. He moved quickly, and knowing the only way to stop the Risen was to destroy their heads, extracted his cutlass, and rushed after the unliving monster. He found him standing on the fallen girl, holding his blade with both hands to deliver a final stab at the hapless woman.

She had clearly slipped on one of her shoes, her ankle had failed to support her, and had fallen face first on the floor. Now, she was trying to lift herself, unaware the creature was about to kill her. Yet, she noticed his shadow, and instinctively rolled on her back to face her enemy.

Geist swung his heavy cutlass in a wide arc.

Wendy screamed as black blood sprayed her face and the monster's head rolled away down the slope. The unliving body faltered, then fell backward, hitting the floor with the sound of overripe melons being squashed.

"You're safe now," Geist said, offering her his

hand. She looked at him suspiciously, still shaken by her brush with death, then accepted his offer of help. Just to scream again when she saw something behind his shoulder. He turned and slashed at the new threat, but his blade just cut empty air. For behind him stood the headless corpse, his claws reaching for his throat.

"Vad fan!" Geist cursed in Swedish, then stabbed the dead-thing in the chest. More black blood gushed out, and Geist's sword got stuck between the ribs. He lifted his right boot and stomped it deep in the fiend's abdomen, pulling the blade free and pushing the undead away. Again, the thing fell on the ground. That was impossible. He knew the Risen couldn't function without a head. What kind of evil was this? He had personally beheaded, shot in the head, and crushed the skulls of dozens of those monsters, and never had they come back from final rest. He saw the decapitated being trying to regain his feet, then his keen eyes noticed something else approaching—the other one. The one he had shot. The wretched thing sported a big, burned hole where his left eye once stood, and carried something under his crooked arm: his comrade's head!

Fighting these immortal monsters was pointless, so Geist turned to grab the woman and carry her to safety. But she was nowhere to be seen, having already fled the grisly scene. Still confused, he rushed down the alley, dodging the incoming horror, then kept running downhill. He had to reach the *Banshee's Cry* as it was obvious, Port Royal was doomed.

He didn't see the creature handing the head over to the beheaded partner. He didn't see the mutilated being picking it up and placing it on his neck's stump.

"Once aboard the *Scarlet* ye must sew it, or it will keep fallin,' said the one with the hole in his face. " Ye must be more careful, swab."

"Let's get back. I think the cap'n has grabbed our chase," said the second, holding the head in place. Then, he cackled.

"What's that?" asked the first one.

The mutilated fiend scoffed, then cackled again, unable to control his bursts.

"They think we're Risen!"

****

"Sink me! That's the stupidest thing I've ever done," said Drake while he tried to keep his hold on the flagpole. Luckily, it was a sturdy one, made of steel. Kaya dangled close to him, clinging on the same staff. Below them, waves crashed endlessly against the shoals.

"What we gonna do now? Me arms tired."

"I'm thinking about it."

"What? Me thought ju had a plan."

"Aye. The plan was not getting killed. Now, please—"

"We just traded da rock for da hard place!"

"—Would you stop hen-pecking and lemme think?" Drake finished, feeling irritation at her remarks. Those Risen would have skinned them alive, or worse. She had to be grateful for his quick thinking … or lack of it.

"Me no nagging. Me just think we must find a quick solution. Me no hold longah."

She was right. He looked at the flagstaffs. There was another row just below them, then nothing more. Climbing back was out of discussion. He peeked on the left: no grip. On his right: same. All he could see was the rocky face of the cliff. Suddenly, something coarse touched his face.

A rope ending in a noose.

"Don't be stupid, bucko." The Crimson Roger's guffawing voice rang from the roof. "We think you are enough an old salt to know when to stop swinging the ratlines. We are offering a way out of the … peculiar predicament you plunged yourself into. Give us the skull and we'll let you go—"

"Dead men tell no tales, *hermano*," Drake spat, gritting his teeth. "You haven't scuppered me yet. I'm just dancing with *Jack Ketch* before going for the *Lady* herself."

The rope swung toward Kaya.

"We are terribly sorry, bucko, but we don't know what you are talking of. That gangway parlance of yours means nothing to us." More cackling.

Kaya grabbed the rope. Drake's eyes flashed. "What are you doing?"

She ignored him, and then slipped the noose on the flagpole, slowly pulling at the slipknot until it tightened around the staff. "Shh. Keep 'im goin'," she mouthed. With an acrobatic stunt, she spun and landed with both feet over the pole. Drake had no idea of what she was up to.

"I just said," he yelled to be heard above the crashing surf, "I'm just hanging. Don't they teach you the basics in whatever fleet you serve? Don't you know *Jack Ketch* is the hangman? And the *Lady* is Death?"

Kaya moved stealthily on all fours, keeping her balance on the staff. She gripped the tight rope with both hands.

"Still makes no sense, bilge rat. You aren't hanging by the neck ... not yet." The Crimson Roger's voice became grimmer. "You are wasting our precious time."

Suddenly, Kaya pulled at the rope with all her strength, surprising the thug at the other end. He had winded the hemp around his body and, when Kaya yanked at it, he lost his balance and flew out of the roof, plunging past the couple and ending short of a few feet from the rocks below. Now they had a way down.

"We'll get you, and you will pay for this, scurvy dog," hissed the Crimson Roger, then bolted away, soon followed by his minions, his cackling fading in the night.

"Shiver me timbers!" Drake couldn't believe his eyes. This lass was full of surprises.

Kaya was now slithering down the rope, while the maniac below was going on reverse, climbing up, the rope still tied at his waist. She stopped her descent just a few inches from the goon, then began eating at the hemp with her dagger. The pale being doubled his efforts to reach at her, but Kaya was faster: the rope frayed, and then gravity did the rest. The thug crashed on a jutting rock, breaking his spine. Immediately, Kaya jumped off the rope and sunk her blade into the man's mouth. However, this didn't kill him and he lunged at her with both hands, getting hold her nightgown's hem.

Drake followed her down quickly, unsheathed his smallsword and, with a violent slash, cut through the thug's throat, cleaving his neck. The man's head flopped back, squirting black blood, until it finally tore free of its fleshy flaps with the sound of ripping cloth.

"It's over. Let's go before those creeps show up down here," Drake said, but Kaya wasn't moving. The being still clutched at her dress. The head gurgled something unintelligible.

"Blimey!" Drake was shocked. What kind of creatures were these? How was that possible?

Kaya pulled at her nightgown, but the unliving creature didn't yield until the cloth ripped, leaving shreds of fabric in the monster's claws. Speedily, she hurried to the severed head, placed the heel of her boot on the creature's brow, and unstuck the blade from the gaping maw. The head began to giggle like a wench, chilling Drake's blood.

"Now, bring me ovah t' jur boat. Fast!" Kaya shouted.

His eyes glued on the jerking living corpse, Drake moved closer to her. "Never seen something like that. I think I'll need a long session of kill-devil to blast that vision out of me brains. Y'know what, lassie? Now I believe your story."

****

Things were looking dire for the staunch defenders of Port Royal, as the undead pack kept advancing, cackling like hyenas and blasting soldiers with their grafted guns, stopping only to recharge their weapons, and ignoring any damage they suffered. In the end, even the bravest of the town's militia had to back away and ships began to set sail for safer lands. Even worse was the mass of civilians gathering at *Northdocks*. Panicked villagers did everything possible to get a place aboard any of the departing vessels, to the point of stabbing one another. Kids were trampled, while old and physically hindered people were left behind to fend for themselves. It was just a reenactment of what had happened ten years earlier in now lost Europe. The mists had returned, engulfing the whole town, so the inhabitants had no way to make out friend from foe, and more than one citizen emptied guns on approaching shadows just to discover to have killed innocents. Meanwhile, the higher-ups flocked the Admiralty docks, trying to keep their countenance, but as the first of those grinning creatures emerged from the fog, they too succumbed to barbaric ways. However, there were heroes, too. Bold old captains sacrificed their very lives to save those of whole families. Footpads who took pity of little street urchins. Innkeepers who boarded shut their premises to keep out the monsters and lock inside their guests.

Then, as suddenly as it all began, it stopped.

The dead cocked their heads as they listened to a silent call, then stopped their fighting and slowly slouched back to the sea.

They were no long interested.

****

In the early dawn light, Drake and Kaya ran along the shore at the northern tip of Port Royal. He was just beneath Fort James when he spotted the familiar silhouette of the *Banshee's Cry*. He stopped to catch his breath, then pointed out the vessel to Kaya.

"That's me ship. Hope you can swim."

The woman nodded. "*Oui*, me kan."

Drake looked at the brig's prow as she moved

along the channel. They weren't leaving; they were looking for him. "Let's go," he twanged, grabbing her hand.

****

MacTavish finely maneuvered the ship along the crowd of barges and boats that congregated at the inner harbor. With the help of Geist's keen eyes and much of his art at the tiller, he avoided most of them, yet some got bumped by the larger ships and capsized.

"Smart there with the riggings! We're scudding too much," he yelled, and all hands scrambled to their posts. Mac was feeling her. He had become part of the ship, like he was physically connected to the wooden vessel. He felt the helm in his hands, the grumble of the decks under his feet, and the whoosh of the waves sliding by the hull. He knew everything about her. Yet, he wasn't using his eyes, for he had little interest in what he saw. He had given over that part to Geist and followed his precise directions from the crow's nest. Yet, he scanned the ground for his captain.

"Can't see him," said Red Leg, who was standing by him. The Admiral had taken command of the ship and was looking frantically to reach his mansion's secret dock. Because just below the fortress-like building, there was a cave. He'd had it dug out and connected to his manor by means of an iron stair. Large enough to host

O'Neill's private barge, the cave had two massive front doors painted to look like the uneven surface of the cliffs.

"There he is!" Geist shouted from the nest.

Mac turned his head toward the spot the albino was pointing at and caught sight of the familiar figure of Drake standing at the shoreline with the black woman. "Throw a line," he snapped to Red Leg. The Admiral descended the castle and rushed starboard, but Luther had done that already.

MacTavish saw Drake grab it, bind it twice around him and the girl, and tug at it to signal he was ready. Immediately, the large German yanked them off their feet, dragging them into the frothing waters. "Hoist them up smartly!" Mac was worried they could drown.

They were halfway to the *Banshee* when a huge frigate emerged from the mists coming close to collide with the brig, had not Mac veered portside. "Come off it! Heave to port!"

The dark ship sliced through the waters, catching the rope under the keel, causing Drake and Kaya to be pulled underwater.

Then, the rope snapped.

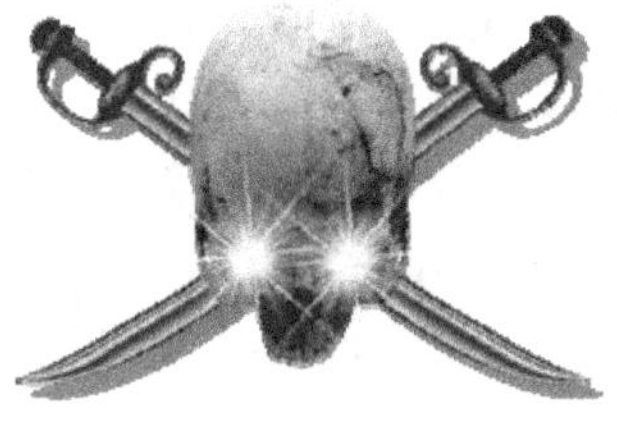

CHAPTER EIGHT

THE SCARLET WITCH

The tall ship's hull looked all black in the mists, but in truth, she was a dark crimson color, stained with black spots. A frigate of English make, she was one of the few warships built of that size. Measuring more than one hundred and fifty long, with a single gun deck holding forty cannons, she sported a large castle on the stern with a wide poop above the quarterdeck. Three-masted and square-rigged, her sails were also crimson and a black flag—with a flaming red _Jolly Roger_—fluttered above the empty crow's nest. Yet, what chilled the blood in the onlooker's veins were her ghastly decorations. Just below the bowsprit, a somewhat preserved skeleton was nailed to the hull, its jaw open in an everlasting scream. Bones of all types and sizes trimmed the railings, while rings of shrunken heads adorned her masts like hellish garlands.

The _Scarlet Witch_ was a horror to behold.

****

Drake saw the ship before it impacted with the line and, instinctively, filled his lungs and held his breath. The vessel's keel hit the rope and rapidly slid underside it, dragging them both forward. A vortex of frothing bubbles hampered his vision, while he struggled with his scabbard to draw the blade. Finally, he succeeded, but the rope snapped before he could act and the sudden change in momentum caused him to lose grip of the sword, causing it to spiral down the dark abyss. Ignoring the weapon, he looked for Kaya, but couldn't see her, so he swam farther until he spotted the scrambling woman. She had been surprised by the unforeseen dive and had clearly swallowed seawater. Quickly, Drake thrust his body forward.

Kaya stopped moving and began to drift down.

In panic, he doubled his effort and dived in the dark, hands extended. He couldn't see anything, but soon his right hand felt the soft texture of her nightgown and he yanked at it. The unconscious woman pulled closer; he wrapped his left arm around her waist, and then quickly made for the surface. Drake emerged, his own lungs hungry for air. He kept Kaya's head out of the water and looked at her face. No signs of life. Desperate, he spun around, evaluating distances. The shore was within his reach.

Then, the girl's unmoving body was pulled off his grasp as something hoisted her aloft like a sail in the wind.

Taken aback, he could do nothing except watch as Kaya vanished aboard the dark vessel while it made for open waters and the purple glow of coming dawn.

****

Kaya awakened inside a dark place.

And she saw the leering, hangman-like eyes shining above her.

She screamed, but the creature put a dirty hand on her mouth, muffling her shrill. At his stinking touch, she tried to lift her arms to push that disgusting being off, only to find them tied down, restrained by leather bounds. She struggled, pulling at the ties, and the monster began to cackle, amused by her distress. Soon, she had to give up; there was no way to get free. When she finally relaxed, the pale-skinned creature released his hold of her mouth and pulled away, fading in the dark. However, she could still feel his presence there, as his stench lingered in the air.

Abruptly, the warm golden light of a lantern brightened the room, and Kaya could finally see her surroundings. Bound to a queen-sized bed's heavy frame, with no mattress on it as she could feel the hardness of the wooden planks under her back, she lay spread-eagled, her wrists and ankles restrained by leather bounds to tall posts. She had to lift her head to see her captor. He was a tall individual, whose slick, oily hair descended on his gaunt face like a patch of putrescent seaweeds. His thin lips were black and withered, yet pulled up in a constant grin. Weirdly, both nostrils had been sewn shut by thick, dark-fibered thread. The dead pirate wore a set of black-colored clothes, loose on his gangly frame, and from his thin neck dangled a necklace made of human teeth. His bulging eyes locked on her; he just stood there like a grotesque statue. A large lantern suspended from a post in the blackened walls. The rest of the room looked empty and scorched, like it had suffered damage from fire. She had no pale idea of where she was.

Kaya remembered water filling her lungs, then nothing. Yet, the rolling below told her she was on a ship. This had to be a cabin. She looked at herself. She was naked.

"Stop staring t' me, *masisi*." Her voice was raspy, sore for the punishment and the salt.

The gaunt man cocked his head, and then a whispering voice came out of his thin lips. "I see you're awake. Gonna fetch the cap'n."

"Don't ju think me deserve a bettah treatment? Where are me clothes?" She felt more humbled than scared. The tall being ignored her protest, opened a hatch and disappeared below, leaving her alone in the wrecked cabin. But it didn't last. Shortly thereafter, the familiar figure of the Crimson Roger emerged from the trapdoor, followed by the gaunt man.

"We are glad you're finally awake, Miss. How do you feel?" He stepped in the room and she could see he had replaced the scythe at his stump with a lighter hook.

"How do me feel? Why do ju care? Me standing naked and bound among pirates, how do ju think me should feel?"

The Crimson Roger came closer, his eyes two flickering flames. "Cushing, please, go find some fitting clothes for our guest. We're gentlemen, after all." The servant went down the hatch. "And bring some food and clean water. She must be starving."

"Me no hungry—"

He waved her rebuke off. "You will eat. As for that word, *'pirate'*, that's something we don't want to hear again. We are buccaneers."

"Does it make any difference?" She looked at him with spite.

"Yes, it does. We were members of the *Brethren*—"

"Ju said it, ju were. Ju just attacked Port Royal, so, dat definitely sets ju out of da *Brethren of da Coast.*"

The Crimson Roger pulled back. "Semantics and politics!" he shrilled. "They stand to a woman like pigs amidst poultry!"

It was her turn to leer. "*Oui.* In fact, here me see one pig and a hundred hens."

Cushing returned with a set of male clothes under his arm and a silver tray loaded with bread, cheese, and some fruits, as well as a dented pewter cup. In his other hand, he clutched a jug. "That's all we have aboard, Cap'n."

The Crimson Roger nodded then turned his glare back to Kaya. "We're terribly afraid, you'll make content with the meager supper we can offer, my dear. You see, we do not need food to survive. We never starve, we never thirst, and," he ogled her naked breast, "we never feel the need for carnal pleasures. So, you don't have to worry about your virtue. It will stay intact as much as you were born with. Unless, you had that foolish Englishman take it aw—"

"Stop playin' games and get t' da point, ju *souse' zozo*! Why no ju kill me?" she said in anger.

Cushing turned his dull eyes toward his captain. "Yes, why don't we?"

The Crimson Roger ignored him. "There's no sense in killing you, Miss. You are here because you've got something that belongs to us. And we want it back."

She started to laugh. "*T'as oublié ta cervelle chez la putain qui t'a donné naissance?* Me handed da skull t' Captain Drake, no ju remember? Probably 'im lost it or it sank with 'im." She couldn't believe this living legend could be such a moron. His deeds in the Lesser Antilles were, evidently, exaggerated. Yet, her laughs didn't produce disappointment in the monster's face as she expected.

"We know," he said with heavy sarcasm.

"That's why you are here, Miss. Drake will bring us the skull." He raised his voice. "We are waiting for him. In fact, we are sailing at minimum speed, just to give your beloved *pirate* plenty of time to catch with us."

Cushing kept his gibbering expression, yet he cocked his head, clearly confused. The Crimson Roger gestured for him to come forward and place the tray on the floor. Then, he started to pace around the room, slapping the flat side of the hook on the palm of his good hand. "Now," he started again, "we are going to set you free." Cushing worked at her bounds. "However, we expect you to behave as the lady you are. Any attempt to escape will be punished. You see, the choice is yours: you can either live comfortably among us, or not."

"How do ju intend t' punish me? By flogging? Ju need me alive, ju said it. Ju had t' grab jur precious skull till ju had opportunity. But ju had t' waste time with sick games and riddles only jur own empty skull could conceive. Ju are a relic, *duppy*. Ju no belongah here. Me beg *Ghedé* and *Baron Samedi* t' rid da world of jur odious presence. Higher deeds must be accomplished, and ju are just a nuisance in history." Kaya rolled her eyes back and started to chant in French.

"We suggest you stop that now. It's pointless and boring. Your *Loa* do not belong to this ship. They won't lift a finger to save you. Mostly because you just know half of the story." He kept pacing around. "Young Mambo, we were made what we are by the Aztec gods themselves, the same ones who unchained the *Curse* on this very world."

She stood silent and the Roger stopped pacing, then pointed his hook toward her. "You will dress now, and eat. And you will do as Cushing asks. Once you are ready, we'll meet again in our quarters, where we'll account you on the true story of the Plague. And it won't be a bedtime tale, we assure you."

He strode away, going for the hatch, but as he reached for it, he froze, then, with a precise maneuver, avoided something, and finally disappeared into the hole. At first, Kaya did not grasp the villain's move, until she noticed motes of dust dancing in a tiny ray of light. There was a fissure in the eastern wooden wall and a thin line of sunlight shone through it straight to the floor. It had to be early morning. Her eyes darted to Cushing—who had just finished freeing her limbs from the bounds—and followed him as he moved to the hatch. Just a few inches from the light beam, he ducked in the same way the captain had done before, then, carefully dodged the shining line, lest it fall anywhere on his withered body.

Kaya grinned. She had a weapon.

****

Later, dressed as a sailor with a dirty red shirt—

the sleeves of which she ripped off for comfort—and a loose pair of striped pantaloons she'd tucked in her boots, Kaya was taken below by Cushing. The frigate had three decks. The upper one was the gun deck, lined with bronze cannons, but it also doubled as the crew deck, as the ghastly creatures had removed all the unnecessary partitions to allow them to mull about when they could not crowd the main deck. At first glace, they looked all the same, with pale yellowish skin and bulging eyes. Some wore tatters of red clothes; others shuffled around bare-chested. A few were busy taking care of the guns, but most of them had more urgent and personal issues. They were absorbed with performing crude surgery on their damaged bodies. Severed heads were sewn back to neck stumps, bullet holes were plugged with metal rivets, or leather patches. Missing extremities were replaced with blades, maces, or flintlock pistols. The whole deck looked like a floating hospital out of Hell.

Led by Cushing among the undead crew, Kaya reached another ladder at the ship's aft and the ghoulish servant motioned to her to climb it. The hatch opened into a large cabin, lightened by candles, with a dining table dressed with a remarkably clean linen cloth, golden plates, silver goblets, and fine cutlery. A somber oil painting—depicting a grim still life of a skull sitting on a pile of rotting books, a clay candleholder, and an open pocket watch—hung on the left wall, just above a stone figure of a weird-looking dog. On the opposite side, an iron cage held the skeletal remains of a small creature, maybe a monkey. A large desk had been positioned at the cabin's rear, close to the boarded shut wide stern windows, bursting with precious items from all over the world.

On a plush gray velvet chair sat the Crimson Roger. He had removed his hat, and Kaya could see the hairless top of his exposed cranium bone. He stared at her as she came into the cabin, his red irises shining brighter than the candles. "Well, we are pleased to see you dressed up." He pointed her to a chair facing him. "Sit down, be our guest."

She hesitated, and Cushing roughly shoved her into the seat. The woman grunted a feeble protest at him, then turned her attention back to the picture. There was something mesmerizing in it. The Crimson Roger noticed. He stood and went for the painting. "We see you are appreciating our *object d'art,*" he said. "This is '*Vanitas*', a still life from *Pieter Claesz*. A modest artist in our humble opinion. Yet, we take account of the deeper meaning of it." He pointed to the skull and chuckled. "This is a lamentation of the transience of all things. The cranium, the femur bone, and the watch are there to show us the brevity of life. To tell us to enjoy it at its fullest."

"Something dat ju clearly no understand," she scoffed. "Da natural order of things is impermanence, but ju opted t' subvert da balance."

"You know nothing of us!" When he was angry, his voice turned shrilling and pitched, like that of a harlot. "You only know the legend, or rather what your mother told you. And that," he pointed the hook at her, "…that is a lie."

"So, tell me: who are ju, Crimson Roger? Or rather," she gestured toward the painting, "…who were ju, before jur soul was scorched and molded by da Abyss?"

The Crimson Roger returned to his seat. "We promised you a story," he said, his voice now a whisper. "And we'll give you one." The man gestured for Cushing to fill a goblet with wine and bring it to Kaya. The servant complied, but the girl refused to drink. "Too bad, it's a French wine. Very precious. Sadly, no one will palate it aboard the *Scarlet Witch*." He eased his dry frame on the decorated chair. Then, he started his story.

"Our story … the story of the *Scarlet Witch* and her accursed crew, began in 1662. In those times, she went by another name: the *Zeeheks*—the *Sea Witch*. Or so we had rechristened her after our bold capture off the coast of Anguilla. But that's another story, from another life. We were buccaneers, members of the *Brethren of the Coast*, but one of us was a bit different. He was ambitious, having in the past been a privateer for the Dutch West Indies Company in Bahia, and at the time lived among the English of Jamaica. He wanted more. He dreamed to become the greatest buccaneer of all history, somewhat becoming invincible. He led his crew to visit dark places, talked with *Indians*, *Negroes*, and slaves. He learned about voodoo, and the Aztec ways. And he personally witnessed the miracles of *Blood Magic*. Are you with us so far?"

"So far? *Oui*."

The Crimson Roger went back to studying the painting, as if in it there lay the rest of his story. A story about man's own mortality. "We captured a slaver, out of Hispaniola. Our captain hated the Spaniards with a passion, so he had all of them slaughtered at boarding, and those who survived were tortured, mostly by roasting them on a grill of green wood, which the Arawak Indians called a '*buccan*'. And we assure you, it is an ugly way to depart this world. One of the *Negroes*, named Endeley, knew some Dutch, and told the captain something that pitted his curiosity. There was a village, set up by your people, escaped slaves from Hispaniola, right in the wilds of an unexplored island at *Las Tortugas*—or as Sir Francis Drake called them, the Cayman. He told the captain there lived a Voodoo Queen, a priestess of such power she could reanimate the dead, entrap the souls of men, and infuse them with everlasting life."

"The place belongah t' da Kalinago. Was no Voodoo Queen dere—"

"Do not interrupt us!" he snapped. "That's your

version of the story. A warped one. Didn't come to your mind that from the times of Columbus, the Kalinago of *Mabouyacay* had to be extinct when Hackett's fleet reached their shores? They were wiped out by disease and famine. Yet, some of them joined their blood kin in Hispaniola, where they mixed it with those of your people. And yet, dear Miss, that's another story to be told. Suffice it to say, Endeley offered a deal to our captain: in exchange for safe passage to *Mabouyacay*, he would ask the Queen to perform a ritual that would turn the captain undefeatable. And so, we traveled to that dark island and once there, the *Negro* did as expected. However, the Queen refused to grant the captain eternal life, judging him unworthy. She mocked and insulted him; to her eyes he was just heathen scum."

He pressed his wiry hand against his eyes, reliving the scene, and drew a deep, hissing breath. Then he let it fall on the hilt of his large cutlass.

"The captain went back aboard, yet the *Sea Witch* didn't raise anchor. That night, we stormed the village and captured it by means of arms. We gathered all the woman's *houngans* at the village's center. She had quite a pride of them. Something like six or more. The captain threatened to kill them; still, the Queen refused to comply. And she paid for it dearly, as our commander was a man without mercy. All the men had been formed in a line, their hands bound. The captain put his blade under the throat of the younger one. 'Make me immortal,' he said. Yet, the Queen's lips stood firm and tight together. With a swift, pitiless slash, he slit the *Negro*'s throat, his blood rained down his black body and drenched the dark island's soil. We remember his eyes were wide in horror and disbelief and his last glance—full of hate—went toward his Queen, not toward his killer. Still, she didn't wince. So, three more followed the first to the afterworld. Again, she staunchly refused to bow to the captain's will. All the villagers saw the apprentices die, yet not one of them moved a muscle."

Kaya shivered at the cruel tale, but she also felt a note of remorse in the cursed creature. It was there, lying below his vicious cackle.

"The last of the three took longer to expire, so the captain stepped forward and stamped his heavy boot on the man's head, crushing his skull. Then, he ordered us to lock all of them in the bilge." He pointed under his feet, to suggest it had happened right there, in the belly of that very ship.

"More than sixty men, women, and kids were taken here, made to sit in the stale water, and weren't allowed to talk, or to sleep. Anyone who tried either befitted for a beating. They couldn't move, and they had to relieve themselves where they sat. Soon, the place became an open cesspool: suffocating, hot, and stinky. The Queen was taken aside and held here, in the captain's cabin. He had his way with her more than once … and in the most unpleasant ways."

"Ju disgust me," Kaya spat. "Ju tortured and killed innocent people. And ju want me t' feel pity? *Oui*, me do feel it, but for dose unfortunate souls who fell t' your bloody hands!"

"We are not asking for your pity!" He kicked the chair's leg she was seated in, having her bolt in surprise. There was still rage in that conflicting soul, no matter how much he fought it with that hysterical laugh. "As for '*innocents*'—"

"Dem were innocents. Ju killed escaped slaves whose only dream was t' be free!"

"We never killed them. At least not all of them. Listen to the rest of the story and you will know. Yes, we were guilty of our atrocities! Yes, we deserved our punishment! However, the Voodoo Queen's soul was blacker than the inside of *Davey Jones' Locker*. She didn't care for her people. She cared only for herself. Nobody knew where she came from. Some said she was born in a dark pit of Western Africa. Others said she came from the Orinoco River in South America. Yet, we do believe she was spawned by Hell itself, and sent among the Aztecs to spread her evil."

"Dat is nonsense! Dem Aztec gods have nothing t' do with da *Loa*. Dem no exist."

"Do you believe that? As we already said, you're far away from truth, Miss. No matter how you call them, gods or spirits, they are the same things: merciless beings whose only goal is to make man's life a misery. There are not *good* or *evil* spirits. There are just outsiders, cold, distant beings feeding on our fears and desires. But this story is not about them. No, it is about the Curse, and how it came to be."

He returned to his seat. "The sun came up and set before some of the villagers were allowed to leave ship. The Queen was dragged back ashore, to witness yet another of our executions. This time, the captain had readied the grill. Two of her *houngans* begged mercy while being roasted to a crisp, and still she didn't falter. She never spoke. Not a single tear marred her face. Then came the turn of another young one; a robust, scarred warrior that spat on the captain's face before climbing the *buccan* by himself. Something changed in the Queen's eyes, and she finally accepted to perform the ritual. We didn't know why, or what made that man different—we found out later—but at that moment, we had reached our goal. She simply said, 'I will do as you wish.'

"And she did. Yet, soon we found out we were indeed immortal, but all our souls had been bound with that of the captain, and his own soul had been siphoned into that crystal skull. Worse was the fact we were forced to obey her whims. For two years and two months, she said. The *Sea Witch* caught fire, but it was not consumed by it; the flames just turned her into the bloody and scourged thing we inhabit now. We changed her name to *Scarlet Witch* and set sail to the Spanish

Main, to sack villages, and prey on treasure ships, just to recover any arcane item of the Aztecs the Queen wanted. We did this for two years and two months. Then, our bonds vanished and the *Scarlet Witch* returned to *Mabouyacay* for the last time. The Queen had promised she would give us the skull, but she could never give back our souls; those belonged to the gods."

"And ju found she dead? Killed by Hackett?" Kaya inquired.

"No. She's not dead. At least not completely so. You see, when the English fleet reached the Caymans, they pounded the village from afar. Hackett knew it was not a Spaniard garrison, but his men didn't. Once he was sure all possible resistance had been subdued, he ordered longboats to deploy men on the beaches. What they found was very different from what they expected. They had slaughtered harmless *Negroes*. Not that they cared, but King Charles would be seriously upset by having spent so much fortune on a mission to wipe out a tiny village of escaped slaves. Commodore Hackett went ashore, his face like stone while he took in the carnage. But he was still sure devil-worshipers lived there, so he ordered his men to look for survivors. And two they found. The Commodore realized his mistake too late. After torturing the two men for information on any devil-worshiping cohorts, he discovered the *Kalinago* were no more, and that village had been created by escaped slaves from

Hispaniola, where they had been exploited by the Spanish. Hackett realized that sparing their life now would surely stain his record, as the Navy would learn of his mistake. The decision was made for him by fate on what to do with the two *Negroes*. One of the men lunged for the captain's sword and was shot. Knowing what he had to do to save his own neck from the gallows, he ordered the other one killed. No one would know of the error he had made. Except, there was a Walter Upham, first officer on the *Avenger*, part of Hackett's fleet. The Commodore ordered his men to explore the settlement and Upham found *Mabouya's Well*. Actually, the cave was a *hounfour*, a place for voodoo ceremonies, the place where our very souls had been stolen by the Voodoo Queen. And there stood the crystal skull with black onyx eyes. Upham was ensorcelled, and set to steal it when a black woman emerged from the shadows. She warned him to stay away, that the skull was a ward against evil spirits. Yet, the man didn't listen and clubbed the woman senseless, stole the skull, then returned to his captain.

"However, when the fleet departed from Cayman Brac, the Voodoo Queen regained her senses and went down to the village, only to find death and destruction. She saw the wounds on the men's bodies and became filled with rage. Maddened, she returned to the cave and performed a ritual to call forth *Mabouya* and exact her revenge on the killers. *Mabouya* answered her call and granted her request for the ultimate price, her very life. She sacrificed herself, but the *djab* transformed her into the living embodiment of the Curse. A Queen of the Risen."

"Ju mean, she became like a queen of da dead?" Kaya knew he was telling the truth. There was no sense in inventing that entire story. But why had her mother lied to her?

"When we returned to *Mabouyacay*, we found it as it stands today. A place for the dead, not for living things. But we didn't care, we just wanted our freedom. We talked to the Queen and she told us about Upham and the English fleet. So, we immediately set sail to give chase to the *Avenger* and recover our souls. And we were lucky, or so it seemed."

He stood again and this time went for the desk, lifted something out of the crowd of trinkets, and showed it to Kaya. It was a golden compass with engravings of the English Royal Navy. On it was inscribed a name: *HMS AVENGER*.

"This comes from that ship. That's all is left of her. You see, after their departure from the Caymans, a storm separated Upham's vessel from the main fleet. Lost at sea, both Upham and his crew began to act in a weird way, until he, seemingly under the skull's influence, betrayed his crew by sinking the *Avenger* on a reef. He escaped with the skull and was picked up by a Spanish trader on the way to Santo Domingo. All his men sank to their death. Yet, this was hardly good luck for Upham, because as they neared Tortuga, the Spanish trader was attacked and boarded by buccaneers. The raiders stole the ship and marooned all the Spaniards—and Upham—at Inagua. That night, the stranded mariners received a visit from the *Scarlet Witch*. We slaughtered all of them. Upham was the last to die, lashed to the bowsprit of our ship. He's still there should you care to look."

"But ju no find da skull, righ'? Dem buccaneers had it."

"Unfortunately, yes. We looked for it for years, while the world all around us changed ... died. People flocked here from all corners of the world. There was war, chaos. And amidst all that, we kept sailing. Looking for our souls."

"Do ju believe ju can have dem back?" Kaya was thinking of a way out. She had to force this creature to reveal more. He was clearly a *duppy*, a powerful undead spirit, and the only way to defeat it was by knowing its *True Name*.

"No. We know we can't have them back. But we must be the masters of our own destiny. That skull belongs to us!" he screamed. "And your mother stole it!"

Kaya felt a shadow pass over her face. She had left Tortuga with Admiral Red Leg three weeks before. Her mother had given her the skull, warning her against the Crimson Roger and his accursed crew. She had told her that *Ghedé* himself had spoken to her in a ritual mounting: Kaya had been chosen by the *Loa* to perform the *Caille* at *Mabouyacay*. "Where's me motha?"

The Crimson Roger moved again to the desk, lifted a canvas sack, and emptied its contents at Kaya's feet. "Here she is."

Kaya screamed in horror as her mother's severed head rolled on the wooden floor.

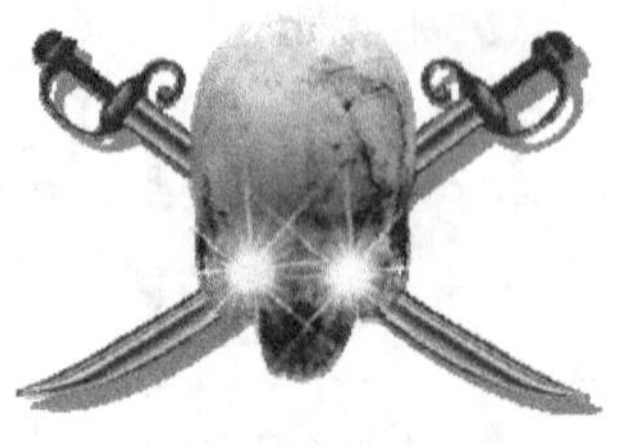

CHAPTER NINE

THE BANSHEE'S CRY

The *Banshee's Cry* was a fine brig.

Often referred as the workhorse of the seas, a brig had two masts, weighted around one-hundred to two-hundred tons, and had roughly the same capacity of a sloop in terms of crew and guns, but could load more cargo, making her popular among pirates and privateers. Usually, ships of this class were arranged with a main deck, and a lower deck acting both as a crew deck—as the hands slept on hammocks amid the equipment—and large cargo area with an aft bilge. But the *Banshee* was different. She had endured so many modifiers, she no longer qualified as a regular brig. First, she had an aft castle, where the captain's cabin, which also acted as meeting room, was located. Above it stood a poop, with a small tiller. Second, the whole keelson had been dug out to make more cargo space. Nonetheless, it was still cramped and uncomfortable for the ninety men aboard. She usually carried a crew of sixty, but the Admiral's takeover had swelled the numbers with thirty of his most loyal.

MacTavish was presented with the spectacle of more than a half-dozen bare asses leaning over the starboard gunwale as the men were forced to relieve themselves over the side. It had been years since he had been witness to such an unpleasant sight. He fumed as he climbed to the poop. This was no longer his ship. He found the Admiral at the wheel, and Drake standing by him; his face was red.

"I want to find the woman as much as you, Red Leg." He tried to hold his temper. "Still, don't you find it weird this ... Crimson Roger just hoisted the *chica*? I mean, he kept asking for this skull."

The captain had that horrid thing in his hands. It gleamed in the early morning. Made of an opaque crystal-like glass, it had two black onyxes set in its orbits. Roughly the size of a children's cranium, it seemed to taint the very air around it with an evil aura. Or so Mac thought.

"I know," considered O'Neill, "but we'll play at his game. There's no other way. He wants us to follow him wherever he's going. And we will." He turned his ice-blue eyes to Drake. "Kaya is important."

Mac approached his captain. "G'morning, sir. I see yer wound is faring better. May I have a talk with ye—" he eyed Red Leg, "—privately?"

"Aye." Drake nodded, then put the crystal figurine in the black satchel. Before descending the castle, he turned to the Admiral. "Think of it. *Think.*" The older man scoffed.

They were halfway the main deck, in direction of the bowsprit, when Mac opened his mouth. "Look, with all due respect, cap'n, I know ye'll not like what me gonna say." He felt embarrassed, but he had to spill out the beans.

"Go ahead."

"Cap'n, ye've seen those *things* are unkillable. How d'ye think we're supposed to fight 'em and win? Let's face it: the lass is lost. Perhaps she's dead already. Perhaps they killed her, or she drowned, or God only knows what they did to her. This is a foolish errand." He was murmuring, unwilling to be heard by the crew.

"She's alive. I know it," Drake said. "I don't know why, but the Crimson Roger needs her alive." He stopped by the mainmast. "And he wants this." He lifted the satchel.

"Oh, please. Keep away that awful thing from me deadlights!" Mac hated the statuette with a passion. Born Catholic, he had an instinctive loathing for anything pagan. Native idols were good only for trading doubloons. "Let's give it to the creep. Who cares 'bout this blasted skull?" He paused, and then added grimly, "'Sides, am 'fraid it won't do. Why didn't he grab it when he had opportunity?"

"Because he couldn't." Drake started again toward the forecastle. The *Banshee* had a small raised bow that allowed for a small storage locker.

Drake opened its small doors, ducked, and crawled inside.

The Scotsman followed him. "What do ye mean he couldn't?"

"You'll find out."

The storage had a low ceiling and was mostly cramped with swabs, spare rope, and carpentry tools. In the lowest part, right where the stern wall met the deck, stood a large chest, unlocked and empty. Drake worked his hand around a couple indents on the ornate lid, then moved it on its hinges three times. Upon a *click*, the bottom of the chest slid aside, revealing a hidden ladder. It connected to a secret compartment. A narrow, concealed room had been created in the lower deck, separating it from the crew quarters. Drake used that to smuggle illegal goods in the Alliance ports, and to hide part of the booty from the League's accountants. However, now it just hosted a middle-aged, somewhat heavy-set man with a ruddy complexion. He wore sober and dignified clothes, unlike the rest of the crew who made do with what best fitted them, and a gray periwig covered the top of his head. A salt n' pepper goatee and a pince-nez completed his *doctorish* appearance. The man was examining something on a tall table, his only source of light a brass lantern hung to a hook on the low ceiling. Hearing the men descend, he uttered something, then returned his attention to his *patient*.

"Shiver me timbers!" Mac almost lost his grip

on the ladder at the sight of the strapped creature. What looked like an old man, toothless and scarred, lay lashed to the table. Basically, a living torso, for his limbs had been blown away and reduced to stumps, perhaps by artillery. But worse was what this man had done to him: his chest area had been skinned, the ribs cracked open and spread wide, and the internal organs had been removed from the cavity—without being entirely detached—and had been stretched and suspended from delicate hooks on a metal post. The top of his skull had been taken away, revealing the gray matter of his brains, and fishhooks pulled at his already odious face skin, adding monstrosity to his unearthly nature. The 'surgeon'—or rather the torturer, as Mac thought—palmed the creature's beating heart with shaking hands. Dark blood was everywhere.

"*Madre de Dios!* What are you doing?" Drake wasn't surprised by the undead presence, but was clearly shaken by the doctor's activity.

The surgeon let the organ go, and it clashed against the exposed raw meat with a squishy sound. "I am running some tests, captain." His cold voice chilled Mac's blood. "As you can see, the creature can feel pain, yet—" he stabbed the heart with a scalpel, "—it can't die." The monster howled, but strapped as he was, and with the hooks drawing out his face, he just managed to issue a low moan. Nonetheless, Mac knew he was screaming.

"What's that *thing* doing aboard me ship? And who's this loony?"

"Mac, this is Doctor Bartholomew Smythe, late of Boston." Drake's eyes were locked on the creature's innards. "He will help us understand those monsters."

"Actually," stated Smythe, "I was born in London. And my full name is Smythe-Westcott" Nervousness showed in his voice as he bowed to Mac.

"How can he? Cap'n, canna see the point of torturing a Risen. They are dead, they eat the living, they spread the Plague—"

"This is no Risen," the doctor broke in. "This is something different. They are not infective, as there is no infection to pass on. Risen can be stopped, once and for goodness, by severing their mind from the body." And to Mac's shock, he grabbed a meat cleaver from the table and swung it at the creature's neck. The monster had just the time to show surprise as his head toppled back, dark blood gushed out, then it detached from the body like a torn sail. The hooks at the edge of his mouth gashed the flesh and the head fell on the floor.

"Sink me bloody!" Mac had seen his share of violence, but this senseless act gripped his stomach, crushed and chilled it, and he fought hard to keep the contents of his breakfast inside. His eyes ran to Drake's impassive face, then, returned to the doctor. He was busy at rescuing the severed head from the floor. He grabbed it by the sparse hair and placed it between the creature's legs.

"Damn ye'll," screamed the monster. His voice grated like that of an old gizzard. "We're gonna eat yer soul!" His bloated and reddish eyes fixed on Mac.

"As you can see," asserted Smythe, "he is still alive and functioning. Now, that's not possible for a Risen, as you know the infection lies in the—"

"Me know nothing and don't need to! Ye're a bloody madman." Mac turned to Drake. "And ye must have lost yer reason, too. Ye brought one of those things aboard!"

Drake lifted his hand. "Actually, O'Neill did. He and his men. I was as surprised and angry as you when he showed me." He paused, then considered. "And also a bit peeved by the fact he knew of me secret compartment."

"Ye can do whatever ye want to me. Ye can crush me head, ye can pull me teeth off, ye can squash me eyes. It won't make any difference, cuz me cannot croak!" The creature cackled from the table. "I have endured everything for years. Me head was cut more than once and still … here it is."

"But you can't regrow one." Doctor Smythe sipped rum from a jar; or rather, he gulped it. He looked at Drake. "I think there is a way to get rid of these creatures. The most effective being total cremation. I suppose they can't actually die, but disposing of the bodies makes them mostly harmless."

"And ye're wrong." The head gritted what was left of his denture—a pair of blunt gravestone-like affairs. "For our soul is immortal and it will drift on westerly winds, looking fer a new corpse to call home. Ye see this? Ain't me original one. Not the one the Lord gave me. Nay, this one belonged to an old sailor. Had been hung by his very neck at *Los Roques* by the Dons when the *Scarlet Witch* paid 'em a visit. Me dunno his name, and don't care, for his *gros-bon-ange* is surely locked down the Abyss or burning in Hell. As for me *gros-bon-ange*, that's locked in the skull ye hold, Cap'n Drake," his eyes darted to the captain, "but me *petit-bon-ange* ... no, that's here and lingers in this body till me has a new one or till the Curse it's lifted."

"Make him stop!" Mac shouted, and his hand ran to the pistol. Drake blocked it and put a finger to his lips. But Mac wouldn't back off. "This is madness! We must burn that thing!"

Drake grabbed his lapel. "Now you lissen! I'm as sick as you of all this *brujería*, lad. But we need to know. O'Neill has it right, Mac. We need to know how to fight this enemy. We made too many compromises, too many retreats! They advance, and we fall back. They spread their curse—or whatever it is—and we fall back. This ain't living, this is surviving."

"Ye will not survive. Mankind's done." The head

crowed and spat blood. "Better to be an Accursed than a Risen, trust me. Unluckily, ye cannot do that; ye don't get the choice. Ye all doomed to serve the Queen."

Drake stepped toward the creature, dragging Mac. "No, we're gonna draw a line here. This far and no yonder! The time has come to stop this all!" Suddenly, he grabbed a dangling rope and a small trapdoor opened on one side of the north wall. Bright light invaded the dark room and a white beam fell on the creature's head. He squealed like a wounded hog as his flesh began to boil and sizzle. Thick, dark smoke rose from the burning skin. "Like it, huh?" demanded Drake. "That's why you had to flee dry land in Port Royal? Because sunlight hurts you."

"CLOSE THE ACCURSED WINDOW!" The head screamed.

"Why? Aren't you immortal? You said you don't care. Your *petit-bon-ange* will simply drift away—"

"—IT HURTS! IT BURNS! WE CANNA STAND IT!"

Drake released his hold on the line and the covering slid back, plunging the room back into shadows, the only source of light being the lamp. The head stopped screaming. His skin looked like meat cooked on a *buccan*: black, crispy, and smoking.

"Now," said Drake, coiling the rope in his left hand, "you're gonna tell us everything about your captain and your curse. Everything."

The creature's eyes now looked like those of a boiled fish, blinded by the heat. "I'll do … but it won't make any difference," he spat.

"Let me judge by meself. Who are you?"

"Me? Me was seaman Samuel Penney of the private ship *Sea Witch*. In another life." His reply came in a cracking voice, even more unsettling now. "It all started in sixty-two, when we caught a slaver out of Trinidad. The cap'n, at those times, was dabbling in *Negro* magic and superstition, and when one of the blacks—Endeley, t'was his name—spoke to him in Dutch fer mercy, he listened to him. Me dunno what he said, but it was enough for the cap'n to let him free and not sell him at the market. And that was unusual, fer the cap'n was one of the cruelest men who walked this land."

"What was his name, then?" Drake snatched the rum jug off the physician's hand.

"He was just a man then, though the vilest one I ever served. Especially to Spaniards; more than once he roasted a Spaniard alive, on a spit over a fire, like a pig. He was a Dutchman by birth, lived down in Brazil for a while before the Portuguese kicked all the Dutch out—that's why they called him 'Braziliano."

Mac blew up. "Roche? Roche Braziliano? Are ye kiddin' me? Pull that line Drake, the monster's lying to ye. Roche Braziliano is dead, eaten alive by cannibals south of the Main." He had had enough of this witchcraft.

"Am no liar, ye ugly swab!" the head roared. "There's no point in lying about this. We call him the Crimson Roger now, and he still commands the *Scarlet Witch*."

"Who's this Rock Braz ... something?" Drake asked.

"Roche or Roch Braziliano." Mac spat on the ground as if the very name tasted as bile. "Aye, 'twas a cruel man, cap'n. Before the Plague, he came to Port Royal and made a name among the privateers by capturing a big Donnish cow, a galleon, and brought a fortune in gold plate. He was a mean dog, ye could see him running through town hacking the limbs off all those blocking his way. He loathed Spaniards and would spit them on stakes and roast them alive, just like the thing said. Having once lost a ship to a storm, he led a group of thirty poorly armed landlubbers in an ambush on a hundred Spanish cavalrymen. He managed to kill 'em all, losing only two men in return. He was more a pirate than a true member of the *Brethren*; in fact, it was Henry Morgan himself that banned him out of the port. Funny story is, he even sailed with Morgan and L'Olonnais."

"Aye, that's the man we're talking 'bout," cawed the head.

"Me heard a story, once," Mac said in a near-whisper. "He was captured by the Spaniards and caged in Campeche. Well, the bilgerat faked a letter to the Don's Governor suggesting that, weren't he careful with his prisoners, all Spaniards who fell into the hands of Braziliano's phony allies would be harshly dealt with. The governor swallowed it and sent Roche as a freeman to Spain. Braziliano soon returned to the *Blue*, where he redoubled his cruelties to Spaniards. He really hated them with passion. Mostly due to what had happened to his homeland. Ye know, the Dutch suffered much under the Don's boot. Well, it seems these *phony allies* weren't so phony after all, 'cause two weeks after his capture, Spanish settlements were attacked and ravaged by an unknown force."

"That's just a legend. Something spread by Roche hisself," the burned head hissed. "He knew the power legends hold. The more people believe a story, the more it comes true."

"Belay it, ye hellish thing!" Mac rebuked. "I've seen with me deadlights meself the tattered sails of the *Black Fleet*!"

Drake patted Mac on his back. "Calm down. There's no point in arguing with deadmeat." He smiled, knowing Mac's sensibility about his reputation of an honest man. He turned to the talking head. "What happened to this … Roche?"

"Oh, he disappeared indeed. For we all vanished. As I was sayin', the *Negro* convinced Roche about something. They went belowdeck for a long time, and then Roche came up and had us set course North and West. There was nothing to be found there—no ports, so no ships, so no plunder—but we all knew we'd be feeding the sharks if we argued with Roche, so we did as he said.

"When we reached the coast of this dark island, we anchored offshore of a tiny, weird village. Roche had us wait until dark, then he rowed in. He had us light two torches on the starboard side of the gig-boat, and one on the larboard side ... he was real particular about that. Said he might be gone a day or two, and we should just stay put and wait for him. Then they rowed in to the village ... just Roche, Endeley, and the first mate. They argued with a local Voodoo Queen, about what Roche wanted from her..."

****

The head told a story of how they had tortured and murdered the inhabitants of that slaves' hamlet, and how the Queen had trapped all their *gros-bon-ange* inside that crystal skull. Drake and Mac listened with horror to the terrible tale of violence, treachery, and black magic, while the physician drunk himself to a stupor with rum and dozed off. The man was already living in his own mental reserve.

Once the creature finished his story, Drake inquired about the skull. "Where does it come from?"

"That? That's an Aztec icon. It represents

Mictlantecuhtli, the Lord of the Underworld and King of *Mictlan*. The Injuns made blood sacrifices to it before the coming of Cortez. However, the Voodoo Queen believes it represents *Baron Samedi*, one of the *Loa*." The Accursed paused to spit more dark blood. "Lissen, me don't know if these gods exists or not, only thing me know is that I'm here, livin' and unlivin'. When me body is destroyed, me *petit-bon-ange* travels back to the *Scarlet Witch* and becomes part of the mists. For days I wander in that fog, lost in it; everything me deadlights can see are the shadows of the other *Lost Ones*. Till me find a suitable dead body. Me don't like the mists. It's pure despair, forlornness."

"Don't ye wish to regain yer soul, sailor?" Mac asked.

"Aye," the creature answered, "but that's no possible. The only one who can lift the curse is dead. The Voodoo Queen killed herself to release the Plague unto this world."

"So, why ye want the skull back? Why does Braziliano need it?"

"Because it holds all our souls. The Queen made us her slaves with it, and the Crimson Roger believes another Mambo can enslave us. That's why we went to Tortuga and killed the black witch. But the skull wasn't there; she had given it to her spawn."

"Kaya?" Drake started to see a pattern in the story. "Braziliano believes she can control you all?”

“Yes,” the creature rolled his white eyes in the skull, sightless, “and nay. Yes, there’s the vague possibility she knows the ritual to bind us. Nay, because the cap’n will make sure this won’t happen anymore.”

“Has already killed the lassie!” MacTavish blurted, his eyes saddened.

“Nay!” the head chortled. “Not yet, he needs her for *Mabouyacay*.”

Drake released a sigh of relief. His boatswain noticed it, but said nothing. There was something he had to ask the creature, something that had been haunting him from the moment the Accursed had started the story. “What would happen should I destroy the skull?”

The head turned his pupiless eyes on him; his facial muscles contracted. “Nobody knows. Yet, lemme tell ye one thing. I’m almost sure that it would release our souls, making us mortal again. The cap’n never said that, but I know enough about blood magic to bet my *petit-bon-ange* on it.”

Drake ran his tongue over his gold n’ silver smile. “One last thing. Out of curiosity. How does it happen the League destroyed your ship and she’s floating again?” Drake had his motives for asking that, but he had to play around the unliving thing’s mind.

“That wasn’t our ship ye blew,” the head blurted. “She was an Alliance war galleon we captured and used as decoy. Our cap’n’s clever.”

"I figured that," he whispered, mostly to himself. Then, a mischievous smile formed on his face. The doctor was snoozing on the floor. He softly kicked his butt. "Sew his head back, but keep him strapped." Then, he turned to MacTavish. "Get back to the tiller. I'll have a chat with Red Leg."

****

Drake and Red Leg were inside the Captain's cabin. The crystal skull rested on the small dining table, above some nautical charts.

"Damn me. I don't know what to do." O'Neill scratched his heavy white beard. "Do you have any idea?"

"Nay," Drake said, glancing at the skull. "You dragged me into this. I knew nothing of voodoo, Loa, and … a cursed crew."

Red Leg eyed him hard. "It's not me. The world dragged you into this, lad. You can't always live on the fringe. Sometimes, you must take a stand."

"Yes, but we hardly get a chance at it." He kept his eyes on the skull, as if all answers were there in that small Aztec idol of weird glass. "You said there was a way to get into the Devil Sea with minimum risk. What's that?"

Red Leg poured some kill-devil from the bottle on the table. His eyes fell on the idol. "Do you believe that story about Roche?"

"I do," Drake said. "What do you know about

this man? Should have been active here when you were sailing with Henry Morgan, right? You must have met him."

The Admiral sipped the grog, gulped it down, then clicked his tongue against his palate. "Aye. His real name was Gerrit Gerritszoon, born in Groningen. He moved with his parents to Brazil while young. He was terrible, Drake. Even for a cutthroat."

"Tell me more."

"He was obsessed with getting a name. He wanted his name to be sculpted into history. And in his late years—before the Plague—he had begun to dabble in blood magic. To what extent I don't know, but there were stories. Sailors said he had been traveling back and forth down South America's coast, braving the Aztecs to look for something." He shrugged. "When Hernan Cortez first faced the Aztecs, he assumed they were bloodthirsty savages, primitive and crude and ready to be conquered and converted. While his views of their bloodthirsty nature were correct, he and the people of Spain soon learned that they were neither savage nor primitive. Indeed, they have proven to be cunning, resourceful, and both willing and able to adapt European technology for their own needs. And I suspect Roche Braziliano was one trading firearms with them in exchange for their occult knowledge."

"I heard Cortez had defeated them—"

"That's what the Spaniards say," Red Leg

interrupted. "Do you want to know the truth, Drake? Most of the gold came into Spanish possession as trade, not as loot. The Aztec Empire is still there, and stronger than ever. As for Cortez … he was killed, and in a gruesome way."

Drake said nothing.

"After a deceivingly calm passage across the gulf, Cortez and his six hundred *Conquistadores* arrived and easily subdued a small village. There, further tales were told of the Empire of the Aztecs and their many riches. Emboldened by these rumors, Cortez set off to bring to heel these Aztecs. Along the way, he formed alliances with some indigenous tribes, for the Aztec customs were bloody and brutal, and their hope was that these Spaniards could indeed overthrow the Aztecs and free their people from their generation's long oppression. Cortez and his small army eventually entered the territory of the Aztecs, but instead of battle, they found themselves treated as honored guests and escorted to the capital city of *Tenochtitlan* and to a great palace."

"Why?" Drake reached for the bottle and swigged at it, directly from the neck. O'Neill looked at him with disgust and Drake just shrugged. "That's me ship, right? I'm not at court." He took another swig. "I mean, why weren't they attacked?"

"Because the Aztec didn't fear the *white man* as their more primitive neighbors. In fact, they had nothing to be afraid of because they were a repository of dark powers unknown even to the vilest witches in our lands." O'Neill sipped at his glass. "A great feast was held in their honor as the Aztec Emperor *Montezuma* came and saw these strange men for himself. Resplendent in gold and precious gems, he struck fear into the hearts of the *Conquistadores* because of his savage markings and tattoos as well as the filed teeth that lined his gums like a great white shark.

"When Cortez demanded tribute to him and for the crown of Spain, the entire feast hall erupted in laughter. Cortez was told that it was *he* and *his* that would pay tribute to their gods. Instantly, a raging battle broke out, but the *Conquistadores* were heavily outnumbered. A small handful was able to escape and remain hidden to see what doom awaited their companions."

Drake sat down and palmed the skull. *What powers does it hide?*

"At the rising of the noonday sun, almost six hundred men from Spain were taken to the altar of the gods of death and had their still-beating hearts ripped out their very chests. Horrified, the surviving members of the expedition looked on as, one by one, hearts were first offered up to their dark gods and then tossed to a mass of priests who fought to take over the grim gifts, squeezing them to drain every last drop of blood into their obscene gullets."

"Are you saying they are like vampires?" The

world was getting stranger every minute, but after he had seen a man surviving all kinds of torture and mutilations, Drake could be skeptic no longer. By Davey Jones, he could even believe the sun was a star by now.

"No. They just dabble in blood magic, Drake." He looked at him with the air of a man giving in. "I don't know if vampires do exist. But I believe in blood magic." He pointed to the skull. "And you should, too."

Drake gazed into the black stones—perfect spheres of nothingness. Absolute darkness. Yet, he seemed to spot something. A swirling mist, maybe? Nay, had to be his imagination. All those stories...

"For Cortez, however, the most terrible fate awaited," Red Leg continued. "When the last of the hearts were ripped from their fleshy cages, Cortez was then given his tribute. Made to kneel in the muck and gore of the altar, Cortez's head was forced back and molten gold was poured down his throat."

"Blimey!"

"Aye."

But Drake's exclamation wasn't referring to the Spaniard's gruesome end, but rather to what he was seeing now inside the stony eyes. He had seen a face. Floating in the blackness, the face had a pug nose, deep-set eyes, greasy hair parted in the middle, a long mustache, and a distinctive underbite. He resembled nothing more than an ill-tempered bulldog. And it looked like the Crimson Roger's face.

"Eventually, three of the survivors managed to reach the small conquered village. From there, their ravings made it back to the Spaniards. Part of their stories were dismissed as insane ramblings, but the portion of the account relating the vast wealth of the Aztecs fueled three more expeditions. Of these, none were ever heard of again. Except one."

The Crimson Roger's face vanished in a twirl of ghostly smoke, soon replaced by something else—something even scarier. A swirling blue-white column of transparent mists coalesced into a series of moaning faces with jagged teeth and blank eyes. Their soundless screams etched into their agonizing faces chilled Drake's blood. The crystal got hot to the touch. He left hold of the idol and it clanked on the table.

O'Neill noticed. "What now? Am I scaring you?" He laughed.

"No." Drake looked at his palm, afraid to find a burning mark on it. "It's not you, but this. I just saw a hundred screaming faces in one of its stones."

"You have seen the mariners' *gros-bon-anges*, Drake. They are trapped there."

"Shall we try breaking this thing?"

"No." The Admiral shook his head. "You destroy that, and you'll release all its wickedness unto this world. And we don't need that, too." He fetched the skull. "I know a lot about this thing, Drake. It has been a cause of trouble even before the Plague. Because this skull must have been in Braziliano's hands before the Voodoo Queen made the ritual. In fact, I suspect she sent him down to the Aztecs to rescue it. But lemme finish me story first." He lifted the idol to his face, yet it seemed couldn't see anything, so he replaced it on the table.

"The Spaniards made an agreement with the Aztecs. In exchange for a tribute of souls to sacrifice to their dark gods, the Indians would give them gold, and gems, and valuables. The fabulous *Treasure Fleet* was built on blood."

"But they are no longer shipping to Spain. The *Armada* always sailed in late summer, but now there's no longer a homeland, or a kingdom where to rain gold. Still, there's treasure around, sailing to *Nueva España* and the Main."

"The pact is broken. The Spanish are no longer trading with the Aztecs. They used to bring *Negroes* and prisoners to the accursed natives, but after the Plague broke in—"

"Red, tell me about this skull. Why do you suspect Braziliano had it before?" O'Neill was well-known in his ability to change tack from a story to another and had to be set back on course from time to time.

"It's about the *Black Fleet*."

Daniel rolled his eyes. *Here goes another story*. The day was marching in, Kaya was still in the hands of that bony son of a scurvy dog, and here they were, swapping scary tales like sailors on shore leave in a tavern.

"In 1508, a fleet of eight ships, all under the command of a Spanish explorer named Don *Guillermo de Aguilar*, set out to look for more new lands and wealth down the South American coast, searching for a likely place to find either natives or old ruins. They found more than they had bargained for. They stole this very skull from an Aztec temple along with all the gold they found. Then, they set sail to Cuba, but they never made it back. Halfway home, a terrible storm blew in and their ships foundered and sank. They realized too late that the skull must have been cursed and as the flagship sank beneath the waves, Don Guillermo heard the skull speak. The fleet would be cursed for eternity for their transgression and they would not be able to rest until the skull was returned to the temple. Then, Don Guillermo, along with the rest of his fleet, sank down to Davey Jones. On the following night, eight black vessels suddenly appeared on the sea, and took a heading toward South America. Don Guillermo and the Black Fleet were returning to that land to give back the skull and hoping to put an end to the torment they felt in their new existence somewhere between life and death. The skull was placed back in the temple and, as the Black Fleet sailed off into the night, the ships began to vanish one by one into a fogbank, never to be seen or heard of again."

"And how come you know the story? That's the stupidest tale I've ever heard!" Drake was tired of those ghost stories. "No one survived, the skull returned to the temple and the curse was over. Red, we must find a way to get Kaya back!"

O'Neill dagger-eyed him. "Insolent. You don't know the rest—"

"We have no time! I don't know and don't need to." He slammed his right fist on the table and the skull bumped. "Tell me about the plan. You said you knew a way to get into the Devil Sea."

"Kaya is the key for that!" Red Leg hollered. "Kaya knows the rituals and glyphs to make us invisible to the Risen. So, we can't do anything without her." He was no longer Red Leg; he was Red Face, too, now.

"We know sunlight hurts them. We could board the ship by day and rescue Kaya."

"Nay. They are faster than we are. And they don't sleep, they just stay belowdecks. They will slaughter our boarding party to the last man!"

"Aye," Drake said, starting to bolt. "But I have an idea. And this time … you'll see." He rushed to the bridge.

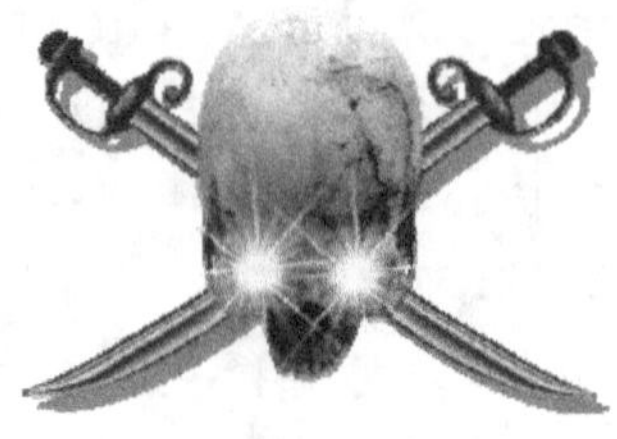

CHAPTER TEN

THE WITCH, THE BANSHEE, AND THE CROW

The *Banshee* had been chasing the *Scarlet Witch* for half a day when she suddenly changed tack and veiled north, landward, separating from the wake of the larger ship. Mac stood nervous at the tiller. He had a true bad feeling about this change of course, yet, Drake was his captain, and he trusted him more than he trusted his own feet. He glanced up at the crow's nest and saw Drake there. He had sent Geist down for a break and was scanning the horizon with the spyglass.

"What is he doing?" Red Leg asked, coming closer to him.

"Hell if me know, Admiral." Mac was worried. "I thought he was supposed to look westward, but he keeps searching for something in t' bay, over there, ye see?" He pointed to a big lump of rock jutting out of the azure waters of Bluefield Bay.

"How can he be sure the Crimson Roger will come for us? What if he just keeps going his own damned way?" Red Leg seemed even edgier than Mac. There was too much involved in this business.

"We've got t' skull, right? Drake knows the devil will come for that." *Or at least he is sure about that*, he thought, but kept his mouth shut.

"What's that rock?" O'Neill asked.

"That's *Harpy's Rock*. Looks like just a big smooth stone from a distance, but that's a ruse." MacTavish shouted a couple orders to the hands, then returned his attention to the Admiral. "It is surrounded by shallow waters, some rather nasty shoals, and a reef. Now, everybody worth his sea legs knows that's no-good for a ship like that." He pointed at the frigate. "A hog like that needs at least a draft of three or four fathoms, while the *Banshee* just needs two before running aground. I think the cap'n—"

"He reckons the Roger will get trapped there? If so, this is a daft plan, for Braziliano plied these waters long before Drake came to the account as a swab. He surely knows about the bay's dangers."

Mac eyed him hard. Had someone else interrupted him, he would not have thought twice to give the offender a good one on the jaw. But this was an 'Admiral'. "As I was sayin', cap'n thinks the Roger will follow, *but*—" he stressed the 'but' "—will stop short of the cliffs. Now, we know they sail blind by day—God knows how they can do that—but will surely give chase by nightfall. I think the cap'n wants to gain distance, turn around the rock, and hide the ship at *Caliban's Cove*."

Red Leg gave a quizzed look. "Never heard about this cove. How's that possible?"

"'Cause actually no one knows about it." Mac grinned. "Admiral, these are hard times, and lemme assure ye, in all me life n' times, I neva experienced so much hocus-pocus in me head as now." He noticed Drake had put away the glass and was now looking upon a piece of paper. "But hard times ask for hard measures, innit? Caliban's Cove was our secret place. We used it to stash away some of the loot of our errands."

"You dirty son of a Scot hog!" O'Neill roared. "You have been cheating on the League by years! I knew it!"

"Calm down or ye'll get a seizure!" He had always despised this man, but now he was really getting on his nerves. "If the cap'n is willing to show ye the place he must have his own reasons, don't ye think?"

"Still…" O'Neill was fuming, and his eyes darted upward, to Drake, who was scanning the bay again with the spyglass. "Fine. Will think about this once everything's over. So, what do you think he will do at this cove?"

Mac spotted the captain stretching out his arms. The signals. Here they were—now they had to navigate amidst the reef and shoals using Drake's eyes. He made the right corrections to the tiller. "Me dunno. And do not have the time, now. Sorry, Admiral, but me need to focus on the cap'n's signals, if ye don't mind."

Red Leg strode toward the stern railings, looking for the Crimson Roger's ship. They were changing tack, too. The frigate was even getting closer, because they still carried full sail, while the brig had dropped much of her canvas. He looked up the mainmast and saw Drake swinging his right fist upward sending it to strike against the flat palm of the left hand. At that, the boatswain—and sea artist—immediately barked orders to lower more canvas. That meant they were getting closer to a passage in the reef.

"Call the linemen!" Red Leg hollered to Mac. "Do not waste time! In shoal waters, coral undersea outgrowths can reach up a dozen from the bottom." The sharp coral could tear a wooden hull like paper.

"Linemen!" Starboard and port!" Mac shouted, then shot dagger eyes to Red Leg. He knew his job. Four men ran at either side of the bow with leaded ropes and started to probe and shout.

"Full six!" This came from a sandy-headed lad on starboard.

Red Leg and Mac nodded. That was good.

"Five!" came the next from portside. Blimey, it was getting shallow. Red Leg turned his eyes to Drake. He seemed relaxed. Then, suddenly, a grin formed on the scoundrel's face.

He had found what he was looking for.

****

"What the hell is he doing?" the Crimson Roger muttered, watching the *Banshee* change tack and head for the coast. He was spying on her by means of a particular device he had developed for the purpose of scanning the horizon from below deck in daylight. A long bronze tube, with two opposite mirrors set at parallel forty-five degree angles, jutted out of the ship's hull and ran all along the mainmast ending with a magnifying spyglass. Basically, two telescopes pointed into each other. The instrument was set at head level close to an ornate swiveling chair of Alliance make. From that position, the Roger had whole control of his crew.

Kaya sat on the floor, and her eyebrows rose when she heard his low disappointment. She looked behind him, and watched as several of the accursed mulled around the dark and cavernous deck. Some were busy pulling ropes and other weird gears. It was obvious their navigation abilities were greatly reduced during the day, so they had developed complex mechanisms to handle their vessel remotely. Not very effective, as they were severely hindered in maneuverability, but efficient enough for their floating tomb to wander around waiting for the next coup. This place looked like an infernal clockwork engine, filled with cogs, mists, and cobwebs.

The Crimson Roger swiveled aside the device and looked at Kaya. "It seems your lover has already lost interest. How fleeting love is, isn't it?"

Kaya narrowed her dark chestnut eyes and pondered the question. It had been a very long night and she had just met that man. Still, there was something inside that kept telling her he hadn't abandoned her. "Love? Why are ju talking about love, when ju know none?"

The Crimson Roger leaned forward, his fires ablaze. "We are not talking about us. We are talking about you. You were easily forgotten, it seems. No different from a wench." He sighed. "Must be hard to digest, huh? You are nothing more than a fancy of the moment to him."

Kaya laughed. "Who told ju 'im's me lovah, *bête*? 'Im just acted in 'im interests. Me no expect 'im t' care about me. \Sides ... 'im has da skull now."

A slightly sinister grin budded across the Accursed's face. "Yes, you are right." He leaned back on the chair. "Enough with taunts. It's time to catch what is rightfully ours." He swiveled back, turning to Cushing. "Let's give chase."

"But ... Cap'n, we can't attack till the sun goes down."

"We know it," he snapped, "but he doesn't. So, give chase to the brig, push her inside that bay till she gets trapped by her captain's own stupidity."

Immediately, all the crew started laboring on the ropes and the *Scarlet Witch* changed tack.

"We're gonna have two skulls tonight." He turned again toward his prisoner. "The crystal one … and Captain Drake's."

****

"She's come about," Red Leg said when Drake joined him on the poop. They could see the crimson mainsails of the frigate billowing full in the late morning breeze. There was no way the *Banshee* could fight and win a battle against that monster. The brig could certainly outrun the warship, but that was not Drake's plan.

"What are we doing here? What you have in mind?" Red Leg's foot tapped nervously while he lifted the spyglass to his eye. "Are you going to fight?"

In answer, Drake grinned then pointed to *Harpy's Rock*. "Yes, but not in the traditional way. They were now getting closer to the rock, yet, surprisingly, Drake pushed Mac aside, and took command of the tiller. The brig changed tack and veered starboard, gaining some distance from the shoal, and got dangerously closer to the cliff.

"In the name of the Almighty, I have no idea of what ye're doing, cap'n." Mac looked at Drake like he was seeing him for the first time. Nonetheless, the old boatswain had served under him for too many years, and a voice inside kept telling him he had to trust his commander. Yet, that trust was being severely tested.

The warship gained, her sails fluttering inexorably in the breeze. Then, she unfurled her canvas, slowed down, and turned portside just short of the coral reef.

"Crap!" Red Leg blurted, stomping his right boot. "Told you he would not fall for the ruse. He knew about the reef."

Drake ignored him and tilted the wheel to veer again. "Release all halyards!"

Incredulous, Mac stared at him. "Beg yer pardon, cap'n?"

"I said, release all halyards, and prepare to go adrift." Clearly, he meant it.

"Aye, cap'n." Mac turned to the crew. "Release halyards!"

Groans filled the main deck, but the sailors obeyed. "I never question yer orders, cap'n, but—" Mac paused to gather courage. "But this way we'll get her right up our bum hole."

"I know what I'm doing." Drake left the tiller to Mac. "Here, have her go adrift. Keep her away the frigate's range." Then, he leaned over the poop's railing. "Luther, have all the guns to port side."

"WHAT?" Mac protested. "She'll list like a pregnant bitch!"

"I know, but we just need to fire on the hull, not on the main deck."

The German gunner turned toward him. "Will we fight now?"

"Fight? Not yet." The captain's attention was now directed westward, focused on something. But the weapon master had no time to turn, because the warship fired an opening volley at the

Banshee. Luckily, the shots splashed harmlessly off portside, but that was enough to have the men run for the hatchways.

"Return to posts! Hold positions or I'm gonna shoot you like dogs!" Drake produced his pistol to show he meant it. The men returned to their posts. He turned to Mac. "Bring her in as close to the coast as you can, then drop anchor. Have Geist on lookout and..." He paused at the look of exasperation in the older men's eyes. "Trust me." Then, he faced Red Leg. "Have all fighters ready. Tell 'em, in case of combat, to hack 'em to pieces and not go for fancy. Have them diced. Use all kinda ranged weapons. Tell 'em to target the head first, then go au corps and hack them limbs off."

He descended the poop and went to Luther. "Should she come for it, throw everything at her, shoes included, but must concentrate fire on the hull. Ignore the main deck, there's no one over there. I want the balls to open holes in the monster's sides."

"So we're going to fight?"

"Yes," Drake said, his eyes steeled. "But not now. Even if she comes into range, something I doubt, because they'll wait for dusk, hold fire. I dunno how many men are aboard that ship, but I suspect they fairly outnumber us four to one." He pointed stern and stem. "Give your best marksmen a musket and put them on the castles. Keep an eye on Red Leg's men, for they are untrustworthy. Separate them, if necessary." He moved to the forecastle. "Tell the riflemen to blow them heads off and stay put. Have the fighters go for melee, but only after those things are eating dust. Do not engage them in close combat till they are down. No matter what, keep the cannons on the frigate. Ignore any other ship, understood?"

"What other ship? Are you expecting them to get support?" asked Luther.

"Nay," he smiled, "not them."

****

The Crimson Roger barked orders to his crew while spying on the brig with the magnifying device. They were trying to lure them into a trap—what kind he had no idea—but that was just a stupid delay of the unavoidable. Did Drake really think he could defeat the *Scarlet Witch*? They had the advantage of being immortal; they could survive all kinds of punishment not even the dreaded Risen could stand.

"They're going ashore," he said to Cushing. "Turn her to port and open fire!" He looked at Kaya. "Bring her to the forecastle and keep her locked." All ships were weak astern and stronger on the prow. That was why treasures were stored forward and the captain's cabin was always astern: a captain was not supposed to be inside his quarters in time of battle. And Kaya was the *Scarlet Witch*'s treasure.

Those cowards aimed to drive the *Witch* into

shallow waters. Well, they were soon going to learn a final lesson, because there was no way they could escape out of the bay without facing the *Witch*. Braziliano considered Drake's maneuver. He had suddenly changed tack, then had made route for that bay. Maybe he considered his brig—having a lower draft—had an advantage in shallow waters, but to what use? He scanned the surroundings. The bay was quite large, with sandy beaches on the north and high cliffs to the east. The water was deep at the mouth, but it turned shallow along the coast, making for an unpractical berthing place. No, that impudent rogue had no purpose of bringing the battle to the ground. Couldn't be...

Flames flickered into his eyes. "Release halyards! Now!"

It was too late. The frigate shivered at first, scraping the coral reef outcroppings, then a loud crack resounded and the vibration reached the upper decks. "Heave to port! Keep soft on the tiller or it's gonna snap the rudder. Keep our damn ship goin'!"

The ship rocked, then tilted slightly to port, and a sharp crack signaled the vessel had snapped the coral head and got free. Nonetheless, they were in the middle of the reef, with no possibility for a lookout. Not in daylight.

"Check for damage! Run the pumps, you lowly cockroaches!" He wasn't worried about sinking; the *Scarlet Witch* had taken worse damage than coral scraping in all these years. No, what truly worried the Crimson Roger was the fact he couldn't understand Drake's plan. Was he really running with his tail between his legs?

He cursed the sunlight then returned to the spying device. The *Banshee* was going steady adrift for the beach and was now coming about, showing her starboard. They were more than a mile away from the *Witch* and her men were scuttling around like maddened fleas on a scrub dog, then a splash signaled they had dropped anchor. Soon followed by a second one thrown astern and the sailors began to tug at the line, slowly lining the ship to the shore. But for what? Were they disembarking? Yes, Drake wanted to bring battle ashore. Pitiful. All he had to do was to stay out of range, wait for the night, then send his crew for a stealthy underwater raid. The *Witch* couldn't get in, but they couldn't get out. He had just to wait for dusk. Still...

"Ship is safe," Cushing said. "The woman is locked and the carpenters are patching the hull. What are we gonna do now?"

The Crimson Roger pushed away the device. "We can't move. Not now. We risk a serious breach and that would be stupid. We'll wait for darkness, then—" he rose from his seat and passed an arm around the gaunt boatswain's shoulders, "—you'll lead the men for an underwater boarding party, but not all of them. Leave the best sailors aboard to help the *Witch* get out of this reef. We intend to bring her around the rock and approach the brig from west."

"So, we are going to wait."

"Indeed, Cushing. Indeed."

****

At the sight of the frigate getting stuck in the reef, the *Banshee*'s crew became jubilant, and started to shout and cheer. However, Drake did not join; on the contrary, he stood on the forecastle and watched them sternly. Then, he produced his pistol and released a shot in the air, calling for attention. The liveliness immediately stopped and all eyes turned to the captain.

"What are you celebrating, scurvy dogs? Do you think they're trapped? Do you think they will retreat?" His face was stony. "Lemme tell you the truth, landlubbers. We are the trapped ones. They are essentially blockading the bay: they can't get in—not now—and we can't get out. They will wait for the sun to go down, then, they'll crawl out of the sea like crabs at low tide. And you will face this enemy in melee. An enemy who can't die."

One crewmember, a young lad with dark hair, stood. "So why did ya bring us here? To die?"

Drake smirked. The boy was brave. "Nay. You are here because I saw an opportunity." He pointed to the frigate. "Those things are vulnerable to sunlight. They become weak and boil worse than lobsters in a pot. So, get ready, because we're going to give 'em a tan."

The men yelled in anticipation as he looked in the spyglass. Yes! She was coming. He knew she couldn't stand any kind of intruder in her territory, especially if this intruder was Drake. One of her lookouts had spotted the *Banshee* from the moment they had braved the reef and had surely reported his presence to his mistress. And now her ship was growing on the horizon, just behind the *Scarlet Witch*.

A large, three-masted merchant vessel, a pinnace of sturdy construction and resembling a miniature version of a race-built galleon of the Spanish armada. Her hull was painted black with two red dots just under the bowsprit, and her sails were also black. From that distance, it was impossible for Drake to spot her commander, but he was sure she was standing on the bowsprit ready for battle. She had surely rounded *Harpy's Rock*, sliding silently in the bay waters, ignoring the dangers of the reef, and was stealthily swooping on her prey like a raptor. Drake smiled at that sight, then turned to his crew.

"Weigh anchor! Hoist the sails smartly. We're goin' to hull that bitch!"

The sun was coloring the sky in bright orange hues while the *Banshee's Cry* left the safety of the natural harbor and stemmed the tide to bring battle to the cursed ship. Just past midday, the air was hot and humid, and the pitch on the timbers was softening. The brig listed visibly on the port side, but Mac was able to sail her—they had moved most of the cargo on top, lashing it on the starboard railing. Lines and braces had been doubled, so that if some were cut, the others would guarantee maneuverability to the ship. Tissues—from blankets to padding—soaked in seawater had been tied along the rails and bulkheads as a protection against flying splinters. Netting was spread above the deck to catch eventual falling spars and sailors constantly washed the main deck to reduce the dangers of fire. They were ready for battle, and also eager for it. Some of these men had lost friends, lovers, or even such trivial a thing as a hard gained shore leave. They had fought against a stranded Spanish cargo ship only to get back empty-handed. They were nervous, scared, and angry.

Drake knew all of this. And he also knew they had to end it here and now, before the sun disappeared below the horizon. Yet, something else tortured his mind. He hoped the Crimson Roger had put Kaya in a safe place, probably the captain's cabin. Worried, he approached the gun master. "Luther, I want the brass to punch large holes in the hull. Do not go for the castles or the cabins; just target the gun deck. Have 'em eat as much wood as they can. I want sunlight to shine inside that floating tomb."

Luther nodded. "Aye. But that could not be enough. That bitch is thick."

"That's why I need your help, matey." He

winked. "Remember that trick we used on that Alliance ship?"

"You want me to… Oh, no—"

'Oh, yes."

"The crew won't be happy…"

"I know, but there's no other way."

"Aye. I'll go fetch the rum."

Drake watched the large man disappear below deck, then joined O'Neill on the poop. "Get your men ready for boarding."

Red Leg looked at him, but his eyes were absent, like he was pondering something. "Did you hear me? I said, get your—"

"They are, Drake! They are!" Red Leg shouted. He was nervous and hiding something, Drake could sense it. "Do you have the skull with you?"

"Yes, but…"

"Once we board that ship you must look for Kaya and make sure she has it in her hands." He scratched his beard, then murmured, "The plan was not really this, but we'll make do with what we get."

"What do you mean?" Drake didn't like the sound of that last statement.

"Remember I told you there was a way to sail into Risen waters safe and unseen?"

The crew was busy on the main deck, surly and grim in the hot sun. Drake looked at them in worriment. "Yes, but you never explained to me. Nor did Kaya."

They were getting closer to the Accursed

warship and soon they would be in range, but there was no activity; the ship simply stood there, bobbing like a cork in a barrel. It looked dead, and her macabre decorations just added to the dread.

"I lured the Crimson Roger," Red Leg said abruptly.

'WHAT?"

O'Neill snorted. "Yes. The Accursed can travel freely into the Devil Sea. Yet, the Crimson Roger would never side with us. He doesn't care about the Plague, and this state of things benefits him greatly." He leaned on the rail. "When I first met Maleah, she told me about the skull and the power it had on the Accursed. A powerful Mambo can control their souls. And with their souls we can reach *Mabouyacay*."

Drake grabbed his arm. "You … used Kaya?" He felt his rage growing. He had never trusted Red Leg, but this…

"Yes. Partly." His face was unmoving, stoic. "I knew the Crimson Roger has a way to get information in all ports. So, I spread the rumor about Maleah having his precious skull. Then, I brought Kaya to Port Royal. I thought the League militia would be enough to stop him while Kaya performed the ritual of binding. But things did not go as planned—"

"Planned?" Drake grabbed O'Neill by the throat, and quickly pressed his cutlass on it. "I should kill you now, you lousy *perro*. You sacrificed your own people for your goals. We are expendables in your personal crusade, innit?" He gritted his teeth, then lowered his voice. "But I won't kill you now, for I prefer to have you live with the weight of your actions." Drake lowered the blade.

O'Neill coughed, then adjusted his collar. "Yes. You are all expendables in this war. And this is not my crusade, bucko, but the last best hope for humanity. Yes, everybody is expendable, me included." He leaned against the railing. "This is war, Drake. And in a war, a man has to do whatever it takes to win. Because winning is surviving."

"None of my men will board that ship," Drake said abruptly. The frigate was getting closer. "Your men will get the honor, and you will lead them."

"You need me here!" O'Neill protested.

"No. I don't need you anymore. You're gonna regret I didn't kill you." He tried to hold his temper, but the thought of all those innocent citizens dead, the thought of the only place he considered home destroyed, the thought of Kaya being used worse than a swab, all these thoughts coalesced into a red rage. And he punched the man in the stomach.

It was at that moment that the *Scarlet Witch* opened fire.

****

After the tension of the reef crash, the crew of the

damned mulled about, waiting for nightfall. From his seat, the Crimson Roger watched the brig coming toward them in an unexpected change of tactics. The League vessel was now less than a half-mile away. This man must be crazy, he thought, to come straight for their frigate. That was an inconsiderate and worthless attempt. He saw the brig was strangely listing on the port side and tried to magnify the lenses to get a closer look, but the device refused to focus.

"What are they doing, cap'n?" Cushing asked behind him.

He shook his head. "We don't know." And this enraged him greatly. He watched as the ship came so close that he could hear the shouted commands aboard, drifting to him in the hot sunlight. A frenetic activity occurred on the bridge. "They are coming for us, but their gunports are closed."

"Makes no sense," Cushing said. "Drake brings her to the beach, then comes back at firing range. He must have lost his reason."

"And what about the rest of his crew? Do you think they will allow him to lead them into slaughter?" He tried to focus again, but his sight was hampered by the ship's bowsprit. She was turning.

"Perhaps they want to parlay?"

The Crimson Roger's eyes flickered as he saw the port side slowly turning toward his ship. She was bristling with a row of cannons. "She's lining up a broadside! Hoist anchor. All men to the gallery. Now!" A desperate move? Or did he know about their weakness?

Cushing sighed. "Should they expose us to the sun—"

"This won't happen! We are going to sink them now! Get our ship moving!"

"There's another problem, cap'n," Cushing muttered. "Somehow, the girl escaped her confinement."

Braziliano, or what was left of him, turned toward Cushing. "What?"

"Yes. One of the sailors was found beheaded and the door ajar. She must be hiding somewhere."

With a scream of rage, the Crimson Roger swung his scythe-like blade and plunged it deep inside the boatswain's belly, then dragged the man toward his grinning face like a hooked fish. "Get her. Get her or we'll have you trade place with Upham's skeleton out there. You'll be the *Witch*'s new figurehead for eternity."

"A-ye, cap'n," Cushing stuttered.

Then, several iron balls struck the frigate on her starboard side, splintering wood and sending it whistling through the air. The Crimson Roger was suddenly engulfed in a world of chaos as his men screamed in anguish and the hateful sun brightened parts of the lower deck.

"Carpenters! Ready to close the breach! Hoist the panels!" They were prepared for situations like this. He left hold of his boatswain and ignored a seaman who had been surprised by the light and was now writhing and screaming in pain, clutching his face, smoke billowing between his fingers. "That wasn't from Drake's ship!" roared the Crimson Roger.

Cushing watched his dried innards, pushed them inside the slash, and then rushed to one of the holes, carefully avoiding the rays of light. "It's another ship, cap'n. Looks like a pinnace or a sloop. Those were shots from culverins, not cannons."

The Crimson Roger's rage exploded. "FIRE! FIRE AT BOTH SHIPS!"

****

The first volley from the Accursed warship whistled overhead; one of the balls grazed the one of the topsail spars, but none caused serious damage.

"Blimey, that was high!" Luther roared in satisfaction.

"Come about! Ready for a broadside," shouted Drake to the hands, but his voice was smothered by the sound of gunfire and he turned toward the warship. A burst of iron shot screamed across the waters and battered the *Scarlet Witch*. The frigate shuddered under the assault, jagged holes appeared along her hull, and she began to list to starboard. Smoke filled the air engulfing both the frigate and the approaching brig as Drake squinted to see through the vapors and the haze. Yes, she had opened fire on them.

"Shiver me timbers! What was that? We didn't open fire yet." Luther was standing on his side, his right boot on a small keg.

Drake turned and grinned. "In fact. That was what I was waiting for. Now, it's our turn to fire."

The German's eyes brightened, then moved to the gunners. "Fire!"

The brig rocked madly as all ten of her cannons exploded in a volley. The impact knocked the Accursed vessel laterally in the water, swinging the stern aside. The momentum sent the ship impacting with a coral outgrowth, and she trembled, then stopped bobbing as she became entrapped in the reef. Damage wasn't as effective as he had expected, but having deprived her of her maneuverability was a boon he hadn't anticipated.

"Reload! Hit the hull!" he shouted.

He spotted the pale figures scuttling belowdecks like skittering rats. Some of them were clutching their face, to protect their eyes from the hated sunlight, and smoke issued from their cadaverous bodies. There was much confusion aboard the enemy vessel, and Drake knew he had bought enough time to recharge his guns. Yet, some of the monsters staunchly held position behind the brass and fired. One of the brig's cannons took a direct hit and was flung backward, fell on a sailor and pinned him down, crushing both legs. A second ball struck one of the gunners, cutting his body in half and sending the upper part flailing through the air. The poor man screamed and rolled in pain before his suffering was cut short by one of Red Leg's men. Grayish matter spattered the wooden deck as the merciful gunshot destroyed his head.

More balls flew through the space between the two ships, but soon another conflagration came from beyond the frigate. The broadside from the mysterious ship almost ate away the *Scarlet Witch*'s starboard side, and parts of the main deck, freed of its supports, crumbled miserably down like friable English pastry. Attacked from both sides, the undying creatures unloaded all their cannons blindly. Used to stealthy raids and their nighttime superiority, the soulless men fought desperately, like ants defending their hive. The *Scarlet Witch*'s cannons roared from both sides and more black smoke filled the bay. The deck of the *Banshee's Cry* shivered under Drake's feet as the frigate's balls ripped into her hull. Splinters, the size of javelins, soared through the air, hewing a path of destruction across the brig's crowded deck, but some were caught by the soaked padding and the overhanging nets.

Drake coughed as thick, black smoke stung his throat, barely aware of the sailor writhing at his feet. A large splinter had impaled through the mariner's cheek and upward though his brains.

He thrashed badly on the timbers before shock took him out. "Rope that bitch!" Drake ordered. At that, a dozen hooks arched though the air and over the larger ship's railings. The planks of both ships groaned as the two vessels ground together, carried by the impetus of their enormous bulks. At the same time, Red Leg and his riflemen opened fire, surprising the exposed—and thrashing—accursed. With astonishing accuracy, they picked off all the heads that came into view, and soon many of the monsters were writhing on the floor like wounded snakes. Meanwhile, fires had started to appear on both the upper and lower decks, slowly eating the thick wood.

Luther did as the captain had ordered him and, braving the enemy's gunshots, half-blinded by smoke, and confused by the battle, lifted the rum keg over his head and sent it crashing amidst the flames. Immediately, the alcohol caught fire and the little barrel exploded, spreading more fire on the frigate. At Drake's word, he and his fighters swarmed over the *Scarlet Witch*, down into the shadowy below deck, and into a wall of cutlasses, pikes, and hooks. The accursed lines wavered and broke as the shock of the assault hit them in full and the *Banshee's Cry*'s men hacked all those lying on the floor, removing their limbs and parting heads from necks. Still, the creatures kept living, and hands and teeth tried to get a hold of their assailants.

Drake hacked left and right, frantically

advancing through the Scarlet Witch's devastated decks, looking for Kaya. Amidst the gunshots, the screams of the wounded, and the clang of steel, he heard the sound of more men joining the fray from starboard. The pinnace's pirates were boarding, too. He ignored them and advanced through a hail of musket shot, right under the mizzenmast anchoring, then climbed a small ladder to reach the captain's cabin. He opened the hatch and found himself in a darkened room. No ball had hit the aft castle, as he had requested, and luckily, the captain from the other ship had done the same concentrating fire on the frigate's hull. He shook the sweat off his eyes and gripped his cutlass tight ready to face the Crimson Roger, but he wasn't there. Nor was Kaya.

Swearing under his breath, he stormed toward the door, but before he could reach it, the cursed captain emerged from the dark and slashed at his back with his scythe. Drake yelped in pain as the wicked blade scarred his flesh and tore away a long strip of his leather doublet.

"Drake," the Crimson Roger said, laughing. "We will feed your hacked flesh to the sharks."

Drake turned rapidly and parried another blow with his cutlass. "You must first kill me," he spat, gritting his teeth, then lunged low, hoping that he would follow the line of his attack with a parry. The Crimson Roger's cutlass came down, falling into his ruse, and as soon as his guard faltered, Drake twisted his wrist and changed angle, plunging his blade into the Crimson Roger's belly. The undead thing groaned, looked down at the metal in his flesh, surprised by Drake's fencing skills, then grinned to him.

"Problem is," he threw aside his own cutlass and grabbed the impaling blade with his free hand, "...you can't kill what is already dead!" Quickly, he kicked Drake in the belly, having him lose grip of the handle, and sending him crashing on the floor.

The Crimson Roger loomed over him. "Are you afraid, matey? Are you afraid to die?" He raised his scythe ready to slash at the fallen man's throat.

Bright light exploded into the room as the wooden cabin's door burst open outlining the silhouette of a lithe but athletic figure. The intruder immediately fired the crossbow he was holding and caught the Crimson Roger straight into the left eye, sending him backward, more by surprise than the impact. Quickly, Drake slithered toward his cutlass and tried to grab it, but a black boot stomped on the blade, pinning it. He turned his face toward the newcomer, who was standing above him. Slowly, the features came into view in the haze caused by the sudden intrusion of the sun.

The woman—for she was a woman—had a pretty, innocent-looking face, more akin to a lady of the court of Philip of *Nouvelle France* than a pirate. Icy blue eyes shone brightly above a small, heart-shaped mouth, lips painted red and holding a constant sexy pout. Her long dark brown hair flew wild under a broad-brimmed hat, and black raven feathers, which adorned the brim, quivered under the light breeze coming from the main deck. Her ample bosom seemed to burst out of a black corset, and laced black breeches—too tight fitting for a gentlewoman—hugged her legs down to the knee, from where the shining black tall boots protected her feet. A purple sash of Indian silk decorated her rounded hips. She held a bloodied French rapier in the right hand and a weird small crossbow in the other.

Drake hazarded a smile. "Thank you, Lorraine."

She kicked him in the belly. "That's Captain Dumont for you, *cochon*." Then she knelt down to help him regain his feet. "How do you dare show your face here against all my warnings?"

He was still fighting for breath when the maddened Crimson Roger sprang out of the darkness and cleaved down on the girl's shoulder, surprising her. Her hand lost grip of the crossbow as the heavy blade carved into her collarbone and she cried out in pain. Drake immediately reacted, kicking the assailant on his right knee and hearing the satisfactory crunch of the knee bone under his heel. The Crimson Roger lost his balance and crashed forward, right into the woman's waiting rapier. The weapon slammed through his neck, piercing it from one side to the other, and tearing veins and arteries on its way through. Black blood gushed around the shaft of the weapon, drenching the French girl's face. Drake regained his cutlass and swung it down on the cursed pirate's neck, and the blade sliced through it separating the head from the body. Still, the creature kept lashing wildly with his scythe hand.

"He should be dead!" Lorraine shouted.

Drake grabbed her by the elbow. "He's not a Risen. He can't die."

Lorraine looked at the head skewered on her rapier. The creature's mouth twitched and his right eye turned toward her maliciously. "We will eat your soul, meddlesome wench!"

Instinctively, she lowered the blade to the floor, then used her right boot to unstick the impaled head from her fencing sword, and the left one to kick away the horrible thing. The head disappeared into the dark area, thumped against something, then hit the floor.

"He should be dead..." she repeated, incredulous.

"Stay back!" Drake pushed the stunned woman behind him and held out his cutlass to parry one of the headless body's blind attacks. Sparks flew as the two blades met.

Captain Dumont forced herself out of the stupor she had fallen into and jumped on the decapitated thing, pushing it down the floor. She tried to pin it, and motioned for Drake to give her a hand, but the being was strong and got easily free by pushing her away, and sending her flying across the room. Drake drove the cutlass through the creature's back; the blade sliced its way down to the wooden floor, effectively trapping the monster like a pinned butterfly.

"I thought I told you stay back!" he blurted. Something moved behind him.

The girl lifted her crossbow and a dart buzzed through the air. It whooshed past Drake's left ear. "Yes I am going to let your sense of inferiority dictate that I let you die."

There was a thump as the arrow buried its metal head into something fleshy. Drake turned and saw one of the devils standing behind him, his right arm—ending in an ax-like prosthesis— still raised. The projectile had hit the creature right in the middle of his bald head, piercing through it and nailing him to the wall. He thrashed wildly, trying to get free.

"*Merde!*" Lorraine cursed. "What are these creatures? And why did you bring them here?"

More of the creatures swarmed from the hatch, avoiding the light and circling around the two. Drake and Dumont stood back to back, blades in parrying position, trying to remain in the light. The monsters cackled and hissed curses.

"To your left!" Drake shouted just in time. One of the Accursed lurched forward and braved the light to grab Lorraine's arm, but she acted fast and thrust her rapier into the attacker's mouth. He fell back gargling, but soon tried to stand up.

"Why don't they die?" Lorraine screamed in desperation.

Drake noticed a couple of the creatures had slithered toward the door and were attempting to close it. He shot one in the head with his flintlock, while the Frenchwoman followed suit by sinking one of her arrows into the other's left eye. But this move cost them both to lose their guard against those in the darkness, and long, bony fingertips dug into them, dragging them into the dark.

They fought tooth and nail, lopping off as much flesh and appendages as they could. But the monsters were too many and soon they were overcome, with hooks and claws piercing their flesh.

Then, despite the loud screams of battle, the sound of rifles, Dumont heard something. A haunting chant: eerie, but melodious. And somehow, the creatures lost interest in their prey and hurried out of the cabin, ignoring the pain sunlight caused to their boiling flesh.

"What's that? There's someone singing in French out there." Captain Dumont regained her footing and burst out onto the main deck. Flames were engulfing the ship astern and large patches of flooring had ceded, exposing the lower decks. The sounds of battle surrounded them, but the melodious song muffled them, seeming to emanate from the crow's nest. Below that, dozens of smoking undead gathered, silent, all their attention directed to the song.

"Drake! Come see this!"

He ignored her. A vibration came from the satchel holding the skull. Something was happening. When he touched it, tiny motes of light twirled in the sunlight and a soft stream of barely visible vapors weakly tinged the air with a rainbow hue. This transparent stream rained down from the mainmast.

Drake was about to join her outside, but the pinned pirate finally unstuck himself from the wall and again swung the blade toward him. He backed away, just to fall right into the Crimson Roger's waiting arms. Braziliano's body had successfully dislodged the cutlass and was now crushing Drake's windpipe, trying to strangle him. He struggled and kicked back like a horse, but to no use. The grinning sailor came closer, axe-arm ready to strike, while tiny dots began to dance on his vision.

"Lorraine…" he gargled, but she couldn't hear him, too enthralled by the surreal sight of those undead creatures immolating themselves to listen to the song. The darkness grew around the corners of his eyes and Drake knew he was going to die soon.

Then, something similar to dense mist exploded out of the undead sailor's body, disappearing inside the black satchel at Drake's hip, and the Accursed fell down like a wet rag. Soon, more wisps of weird fog darted across the air and followed the first into the purse. The

Crimson Roger's headless body released hold of Drake's neck and went down the timbers, too. Drake was free but the lack of oxygen had had the best of him and he collapsed to the floor, gasping for air. Soon darkness closed in on him.

Lorraine Dumont returned inside. "Daniel, you won't believe your very eyes. The *revenants* are…" She stopped when she saw he was dead.

CHAPTER ELEVEN

DEAD MEN TELL TALES

Lorraine Justine Dumont was the daughter of a French nobleman with a passion for exploration. A scholar and eccentric man, Bertrand Dumont moved his family to Martinique when Lorraine was very young and filled the young woman's head with daring tales of swashbuckling heroes and sailing the open sea. He even trained her in fencing, much to the protests of her mother who dreamed for her a safe marriage and a life back in France, but her dreams died with France itself. By the time Lorraine was eighteen, she was an accomplished swordswoman and an able pilot.

On her twenty-second birthday, her father disappeared on an expedition to the Yucatan peninsula. No one knew what had happened to him, but Lorraine feared he had fallen into Spanish hands. It was the year 1673 and the Vatican Church had branded all enemies of *Nueva España* as heretics, so citizens of the Alliance were often marked as pirates and sent to Fort Santo Domingo to be tortured by the Inquisition. Using her new inheritance, she spent a fortune to find her father's whereabouts and when she discovered that a private ship, captained by a Frenchman, had indeed been captured by the Spanish and all her crew had been imprisoned at Santo Domingo, she had looked for the service of League privateers at Tortuga for a daring raid in the Spanish fortress.

Yet all refused. They said, no matter how much she was willing to pay, the raid was worthless because the man was already dead. But she rejected the idea of abandoning her father without trying, so she bought a sturdy pinnace from a Dutch smuggler and hired her crew, effectively becoming the ship's captain.

Although skilled, the crewmen weren't too keen on a female captain and decided to mutiny. Led by Lorraine's second-in-command, a wily scoundrel named Bousquet, they decided to act once she would go ashore.

Lorraine was able to infiltrate the Spanish garrison, but too late. Her father had been killed by the prison Inquisitors and all she could do was to rescue a dozen crewmembers and bring them aboard her ship. But a nasty surprise waited for them in the secluded bay where she had anchored the vessel. The ship was no longer there. The traitorous crew had stranded her there and had stolen all her money. She was in serious trouble as her actions at Fort Santo Domingo hadn't gone unnoticed and the Spaniards were hot on her trail.

Desperate, she looked for a fast way out and found it on a small brig that had been hiding in the same bay. That ship was the *Banshee's Cry*.

Her captain, Daniel 'Drake' Davies, offered her passage to Tortuga—where he was sure Bousquet was going to squander all that easy money—and his services to regain her boat. During the trip, she fell in love with the brig's young captain and they had a stormy relationship, for Lorraine was an unusual woman; she fought like a man and even made love like one. She was bold and adventurous, but these qualities clashed with Drake's traditional mind-set. To him, a woman had to be protected and stay at home, not be plying the sea and leading men to battle. Drake offered her the opportunity to get back to Martinique, but she refused. First, she had sold all her properties to rescue her father, so she had no business back there. Second, scorned by his overprotective attitude, she decided to show him she could best any man.

When they reached the buccaneers' town, the smugglers had already emptied the ship's coffers. Drake helped her regain control of the ship from the treacherous Bousquet, but she stubbornly refused to stay in the safety of the captain's cabin, instead preferring to join the fray. Lorraine was furious and fought like a wild animal, killing six crewmen in the first minute of the boarding. After several more of the instigators fell to her sword, the mutineers surrendered. Some of the crew even rallied to her side, seeing the ferocity of her onslaught. When all was said and done, all the mutineers were slain and Bousquet hung from the mainmast as a reminder to the rest of the crew.

The crew took to calling her Le *Corbeau Noir*—the Black Raven—and the ship became known as the Raven's Nest. However, her relationship with Drake ended that very day and they started a rivalry that was famous in the Caribbean.

Nonetheless, she still cared for him and she was barely holding back the tears threatening to wet her eyes as she stood out of the *Banshee's Cry*'s captain quarters, waiting for a final response from the ship's surgeon. Beside her stood Luther, also in trepidation. He had carried the captain back to the ship, shouting he was still alive because he could hear the man's heartbeat. Shaking, he had dragged that creepy man, Smythe, out of the lower decks, where he had been hiding during the battle, and had '*ordered*' him to bring back his captain. He was like a child who believed those he loved couldn't die.

Both crews, those from the Banshee and the Raven's Nest, were busy hacking off the weird creatures to pieces. Creatures that were no longer boiling under the sunlight. They simply stood there, unmoving. She had told his men to throw them overboard, but Red Leg had cut in, saying those bodies were needed for their mission and by disposing of them in that way, they could only cause them to regain life. She had violently protested, but the intervention of that haunting Creole woman had had her change her mind. The girl was the real force behind their unexpected victory over the undead ship. She was a Mambo, a voodoo priestess, and that chant Lorraine had heard coming from the crown's nest was a ceremony to banish the accursed souls back to that crystal skull. Or so the woman had explained to her.

Lorraine watched the men carrying the butchered cadavers aboard the brig. She still had no idea of what they were doing, but she had decided to comply as long as Red Leg allowed her to get everything in the *Witch*'s holds.

"Are you sure you want that cursed booty?" O'Neill leaned on the railing nearby.

"*Oui*. I don't think it is cursed," she cut short. "How's he?"

"Dan is alive. But Smythe says he could be gone kiddy."

She frowned. "What's that?" All these years spent among English-speaking folks and still she didn't grasp their passion for creating new words or aphorisms.

"It means that his mind could have been regressed to the time when he was a child. Like it happens to old men."

She shuddered, but cracked, "Drake was already daft enough. Won't be a great loss.

Perhaps, he could even benefit from this turn of events."

"Do you really hate him so much?" O'Neill's eyes pierced her.

No. Actually, I love the bastard, she thought, but she just turned toward the sea. "Where's the black woman?"

"She is working on the brig, preparing her for our real mission."

"Which is?" Lorraine asked.

"It doesn't matter," he said curtly. "Just know that we are going to accomplish something much higher than piracy. Our time is nigh."

"Leave him here. I'll take care of him," she said abruptly, then feeling regret.

"I can do that." He turned toward the main deck and spotted Kaya painting the mainmast with red dye. "He's no longer useful."

A smirk of disgust formed on the Black Raven's face. "*Oui*, like everything in your life, Admiral. You discard all things—items or persons—that you no longer deem worthy of your schemes."

He ignored her contempt. "Get back to your ship, pirate. Sack the holds of that vessel, then sink it. I wouldn't use that to ply the waves were I you."

"Do not worry, I don't want that hulk as a prize." She moved toward the port side, then turned. "Leave him here."

Red Leg smiled. "I shall."

****

Drake awoke to the sound of boots hitting the wooden floor, opened his eyes, and saw the ceiling of his cabin. He lay still, only his eyes moving. Then, he smelled fire and started to sit up, only to get a painful streak through most of his body.

"Do not rush things, cap'n," a voice said. Mac came into view. He bent and helped him get upright on the bed, placing a pillow behind his back. "Do you know who I am?"

He smiled. "I thought I was in heaven, but if you are here..." He made an expression of pain as he adjusted on the pillow. "This must be hell."

"Aye." Mac grinned. "Ugly as always."

A shadow crossed Drake's features. "The ship. Is she safe?"

"Smart as ever. Got some damage below decks, but nothing serious. Me thought we were heading for the locker, but ya cracked Braziliano's bumhole wide open!"

Drake couldn't resist at that comment and laughed so hard his ribs hurt. Hell, they had done him badly. Then, he remembered what had happened. "Where's Kaya?"

"She's safe. And lemme tell ya more. She saved our own bumhole." He sat on the bed's corner. "In all me life n' times I neva seen a woman like that. Me dunno how the hell she escaped the demons' clutches, but listen, Drake, she scares me more than the Risen."

"She trapped them souls, right?"

"Think so." His face was ashen, but there was relief in the Scot's eyes. "Y'know? Me n' gonna believe everything now. Even that the Pope in Nuevo Madrid is a woman!"

Drake laughed again, then coughed. "You're goin' to kill me, Mac." Then he looked into his eyes. "Thanks for being my friend, Charlie."

The Scot's bright eyes widened in amazement. That was the first time the captain had called him by his given name. "How do ya know me name?"

He smiled. "She told me. When I was away."

The boatswain frowned. "Who? Who told you?" He was worried the butcher surgeon could have it right. Maybe the captain had lost his reason.

"Kaya," he said. "She was in me dreams all the time. She held me hand and pulled me away from the mists I was lost into." He saw Mac's expression and stiffened. "Still unbelieving, huh? You said you were ready for anything now."

Charles MacTavish nodded. "Fair enough, cap'n." He lifted his frame from the bed. "Do ya think ya can eat?"

Drake thought about it. Hell yes, he was hungry. "Aye, and heartily so."

The door opened and Geist broke in. "You should see this, Mac!" Then he noticed the captain was awake and a smile creased his usually stoic features.

Drake raised one painful arm to Mac, who

helped him stand. The pain was tremendous; he felt light-headed and as if needles shot through his legs, arms, and back. Then it got better. Geist rushed to his side and helped him, too. "Hell," he mumbled, "They battered me well. Walk worse than Red Leg." His thoughts ran to the Admiral. He thought back to the afternoon when he had introduced him to Kaya. He had been so confident, so cocky. And she had been so … creepy. Still, she had poisoned him with her allure. He couldn't shake her off his mind. Her dark chocolate brown eyes filled his memories, sending to oblivion all the rest. He had to see her. Now.

But when he limped to the threshold, another figure came into his view, her azure eyes sending shivers down his aching spine.

"What the hell are you doing? Bring him back to bed!" Her voice was stern, but her eyes were filled with relief. He grinned; Lorraine still cared for him. "I'm happy to see you, too."

"Bring him back to bed!" she ordered, her gaze stating she would not take a no as a valid answer.

Drake turned to Geist. "It's fine. Do as she asks. Whatever you want me to see can wait, right?"

The albino nodded. "Guess so."

They led him back to bed. Captain Dumont came inside. She was carrying a canvas satchel in her left hand, big enough to contain a cannonball, but whatever was inside wasn't so heavy. "*Bon,*" she said, and then motioned for the crewmembers to leave. They looked at their captain and he nodded.

****

"Why did you drag me into this?" Lorraine looked more worried than angry. She was acting tough, but Drake knew her too well to know better. She was sincerely worried for him. The *Corbeau Noir* was well known for her ruthless attitude and apparent lack of emotion. People depicted her as a merciless virago—relentless when pursuing a goal, and cold toward male company. But here she was, worriment in her eyes.

He liked it.

Daniel had fallen in love with this woman instantly, but she was too stubborn, too independent and unconventional to make for a stable relationship. Still, he couldn't lift his eyes off her. Her fair, smooth skin contrasted pleasantly with those cherry red lips. And her hair was like silk. To not mention her generous bosom.

"I thought you could be the only one able to help me. I know you are hunting Risen all over the islands by months. Your exploits at Nevis reached my ears. I didn't know you had a heart."

She frowned. "I'm a sword for sale, just like you." She removed her plumed hat and laid it on the table, together with the sack. A muffled sound came out of it. There was something alive in there. "Drake, we need to talk."

"Still teasing, huh? After all these years. Look, Lorraine—"

"Dan, you can't handle this!" she exploded. "Tell me you aren't going to *Mabouyacay*. That's insane!" She was no longer acting bitchy; she showed real concern now. Hell, she hadn't complained about him calling her by her true name. "It's a trap. I do not trust that woman."

"Kaya?" Now what? Kaya had saved both ships by performing a ceremony imprisoning the undead souls inside the skull. She had proven to be a powerful priestess. Why was Lorraine worried about her? Was she acting jealous? Possible?

"*Oui. Tu es con?* Do you see any other *femme* aboard this ship apart from me?"

Together with *'is that a good thing?'* that was one of her most recurring ironic questions. The first indicating you were acting like a moron. The second criticizing the way you did something. Dan hated both of them. Still, he had to admit he had missed both. The last time he had listened to a *'Tu es con?'* had been when he had lost his secret hideout—*Harpy's Rock*—to her in a fencing contest. They had both been drunk. Drake had recently returned from a successful raid on an Alliance trader and she had just escaped the ambush of two Spaniard patrol cruisers. They were both in Tortuga at that time and the evening at the *Mouette Bleu* had started as usual, with both of them watching each other warily. Then, they had too many rounds of rum and they had ended up arguing, until Drake had suddenly reached out and kissed her in front of her crew. This had caused a prompt kick into Drake's family jewels. However, he couldn't remember how, they had found themselves making love in the tavern's cellar, amidst casks of grog and rotting vegetables. Later, he had bragged about his manly superiority and this caused yet another string of French insults and a challenge to duel. Drake accepted, but stupidly proposed to put something on the plate. So, he had waged his own hideout against her promise to get out of the account. And this had induced a *'Tu es con?'* out of her angry lips. Drake had insisted and … he lost his hideout.

"She is a Mambo. She saved our bottom, do not be afraid of her."

"How did she escape? How did she?" She came closer and took his hand. "Dan, you are a bigot idiot, but believe me, there's something wrong about her. She has a doll—"

She couldn't finish, for a gurgling sound escaped from the satchel, soon followed by the Crimson Roger's odious laughter. Startled, Drake reached for his flintlock on the nightstand, but that move cost him a sudden surge of pain down his back. Then he realized what was in the sack. "You have his head, don't you?"

She nodded. "You must listen to him, Dan."

"What for? Burn it, Lorraine. We don't need his

cackling aboard. We just need his body."

"You are going to lose your soul. You are going to curse your whole crew and ship. For once, listen to me!" She was on the verge of crying and that sight made him angry. Angry at her for being so unruly. Angry at himself for not accepting her the way she was. Angry at Kaya for being so deep under his skin…

"Let he speak, then get off me ship. Both of you."

She lowered her eyes, then went to the table and pulled out the severed head from the sack. The undead thing was even more horrible to behold. His skin had been peeled off by the sunlight, revealing the pale raw flesh beneath. He missed an eye and his mouth sported a deep vertical slash from upper lip to chin.

"We have to say, we are impressed you made it so far," the head cackled. "But this ain't a victory. It's just the beginning of your doom."

"Speak your piece, then be silent forever." He turned to Lorraine. "Plunge him down Davy Jones' Locker. I'm gonna keep his body and soul, but I want the fishes to eat his head off … slowly."

The Roger laughed. "Don't you wonder why we are still here? We were supposed to be inside the skull, with our mateys. Yet, we are here. Talking to you."

"Aye. But I'm not known for questioning too much."

"Dead men tell no tales, right, captain?" His

disgusting boiled fish eye gazed at him. "Well, we are not dead, and we are not inside that skull. But we do tell tales, matey. Oh, indeed we do."

"Where are you now?" asked Dumont. She put the head on the table then stood beside Drake, reaching for his hand. "She has her plans, Dan. Trust me," she whispered to him.

"We are in the mists," his blank eye rolled in the skull, "lost, yet cursed to stay together. Give time and we'll be back, into new bodies. But the mists no longer surround the *Scarlet Witch*. Nay. They wrap around your vessel, Drake. The mists now belong to you."

Drake narrowed his eyes. "What do you mean?"

"We think you're beginning to understand how dangerous that woman is for you—"

"She's nothing to me!" he spat, then noticed Lorraine's stare of surprise at his excessive outburst and lowered his voice. "But she happened to be quite a match to you, didn't she? You thought you could control her, but you failed." He stopped abruptly, staring into space.

"Dan, are you well?" inquired Lorraine.

"Throw him off board!" he shouted, having her bolt. He smiled apologetically, then turned to the head. "You know she can do it. You know she can lift the curse, and without it the Loa will come for your sorry ass—"

"Why is she so important to you, captain?" The head was no longer grinning; its expression turned stern, even a bit worried. "Are you sure it is your head taking decisions? Or is that your groin?"

"Why?" Drake got closer to the thing, eyes ablaze. "Because I don't want you dead to take one more thing from me. You took away everything: the world I knew, me faith, some of me friends, hell, even me sense of duty!" He was roaring now. "I had to leave people back, for heaven's sake! I had to do horrible things, just because of you."

"You are confused. We are no Risen, actually—"

"It's the same goddamned thing!" He spat his words and saliva into the Crimson Roger's face. "Dead should stay dead! That's why we bury you deep or burn you to ashes. That's why we place a heavy slab of stone on your graves. That's the natural order of things. Nothing should last forever. Immortality? Pah! Eternal life? Pah!" He grabbed the head by its sparse hair and put it back in the sack. "I've had so many things taken away from me in me life n' times. Maybe, this is one too many." He limped toward the door, sack in hand.

"The Admiral said to not do that," Lorraine admonished. "Do not drop it into the sea."

"I'm not going to listen to his orders." He turned. "Lorraine, thanks for your help, but you should go."

Her eyes hardened. "That's all of it? A lousy thank you?" Legs spread hip width, hands on her sides, she looked at him until he sent his gaze to the floor. "Dan, that *femme* cast a spell on you. You acted irrational, risking your ship and crew—

merde, almost lost your life—for her. I know you too well … you can't be in love with that *femme*."

"What if?" He returned the stare. "That's none of your concern. I wasn't the one who went away." Looking into her blue eyes was still hurtful for him. He couldn't deny he loved her, still they were too different; she was too unpredictable, like the sea—and too unruly, like his ship. He thought about it. Yes, she was everything he liked, but at the same time despised. Drake had wished for the life of a trader, carrying goods from place to place and trying to make a big profit out of it. Or maybe, being a cane sugar lord, with lots of workers and a nice family. But everything had gone down the bottom of the sea and he had turned to piracy and privateering. At heart, he was a simple man, but first the Plague, then the Alliance had turned him into a man he didn't like. Being with Lorraine would mean accepting all of that, renouncing his dreams. Somehow, Kaya represented something different. She had showed him there was still faith out there, not just plunder and adventure.

"I didn't want to, but had to." Lorraine got closer. "Why can't you accept me as your peer, as an equal, not as a submissive wife? You know I can't be like that." Her eyes softened. "Is that so difficult for you?"

"Because that's the way the world goes. My mother was a devout and respectful spouse; she didn't go around slashing men's bellies. She was sweet and caring—"

"I'm not your mother!" she exploded. "Nor is Kaya. Drake, she has a small doll. It looks like you."

"Go," he said, giving her a stony gaze.

She took off the satchel from his hand. "Fine. But I will not allow you to do such a daft thing." He strode past him, then turned, one last time. "*Adieu*, Captain Drake. It has been nice knowing you."

Drake let her go, knowing that was the last time he would see her. That she would be closing a door he had never shut. He rested his gaze on her beautiful figure as she made her way on the main deck, wishing he could be able to accept her, but inside knowing he never could. Yes, he would not see her again.

But he was wrong.

CHAPTER TWELVE

THE DEVIL'S SEA

Two days later, they were at sea again, but what sailed those waters could no longer be recognized as the *Banshee's Cry*.

The hull had been painted black, some red splotches flowered at the aft and the bow, and tattered black canvases fluttered at every stroke of the wind's. Worse yet were the macabre decorations bedecking the bowsprit, for nailed on it stood a dozen yellowed skulls, clinging to the wood as hellish barnacles. Both sides sported fishing nets, ripe with bones and severed limbs, echoing the horrors at the stem, and arcane symbols, borne out of nightmares, defaced her masts. All the Accursed bodies had been roped, nailed, and even sewn on the vessel.

Kaya had performed a ritual to bind their *ti-bon-ange*—the lesser part of the soul, that thing animating their husks—to the vessel herself. She explained every living person had two souls, the 'essential' soul, known in Voodoo as the *gros-bon ange* (big good angel) and the 'base' or individual soul, the *ti-bon-ange* or 'little good angel'. The first was the true source of life, the soul as understood by Christianity that went to Heaven or Hell when its host body died. The 'base' soul was the secondary spirit shaped by the person's life; it contained that life's memories, likes, dislikes, and personality. When a person died, the base soul lingered on the Earth for a while, and then dissipated—unless its existence was perpetuated through an expenditure of *Essence*. The source of this energy could be a strong emotional imprint (such as that left at places where atrocities were committed), or the attention of living people. Cultures that honored or worshiped their dead kept these souls alive. Yet, some very strong-willed base souls, or those motivated by very powerful desires and wants, such as love, revenge, or hatred, could manage to prolong their existence even without an outside power source to keep them going. This caused the manifestation of creatures such as the *revenant*, or the restless dead, creatures compelled utterly by their one compulsion, their own craving for revenge. Or such as the Accursed, whose *ti bon ange* animated their bodies, but whose *gros bon ange* had been trapped into an *oubliette* of the Spirit World, a forlorn prison of mists and despair. Then, there were the *Obedient Dead*, also known as the Risen. These were under the control of a single powerful entity, which used them as legions to add to its growing *Essence*. In this case, it was *Mabouya*, this evil *djab*, a mockery of the Loa. They didn't feed on flesh, like many thought, but on the living's *Essence*. Risen were always hungry and ever alert for signs of life. When life, particularly human life, was spotted, the creatures let out a loud, droning moan that alerted all other walking dead in the area to the presence of life. As if hearing a dinner bell, the other Risen rose from wherever they may have been and lumbered toward the call to feed. The Risen attacked like wild animals with flailing fists, biting teeth and clawing fingernails. Instinct drove them to kill, bite, and tear at their prey. In the process, these ghouls could swallow bits of flesh, but they were not fueled by it, because they fed on the living's *gros bon ange*. A person killed by the Risen would have his lesser spirit twisted by the Curse of *Mabouya* and would soon rise again as a member of the horde.

So, by hiding the living's *gros bon ange* with the Accursed *ti bon ange,* they would be able to slide into the Risen waters unnoticed.

The silent crew lay sprawled on the main deck, afflicted by a dreadful mood. Fifty fighters, sulking and foul, crammed the ship's decks, while Captain Drake stood by the tiller with a void expression. They knew nothing of this voyage's purpose; still many were obedient followers of Red Leg, and never questioned his orders. Of the Banshee's original crew, only MacTavish, Geist, Luther, and fifteen men were left aboard. Many had died fighting the Accursed.

Drake felt the ship no longer belonged to him.

MacTavish joined him at the tiller. "The Irishman's crazy, ye know? We must do something. This ain't boldness, it's suicide!" Mac would never stop complaining. It was his nature. Give him something he wanted, he would start kvetching about losing it. They just defeated a horror that had been causing fear and loss long before the Plague and here he was, bemoaning on their next move.

Drake nodded, but pointed to the horizon. A pearly and luminescent mist was now coming into view, hiding whatever—or whoever—lurked within it. "I think it's too late for that."

The Scotsman reacted by letting out a curse. "That's impossible! We canna be there yet! Me swear—"

"Mac, the Devil's Sea is growing," Drake broke in. "In less than a year it will reach Jamaica's shores. We already smell its awful decay in night's wee hours. I don't care anymore; it'll be all upon us, now or then."

Then, he shook his head and said, "Handle the tiller, Mac. I need to talk with that woman."

****

Drake found Kaya in the aft cabin, half-naked, standing inside a circle drawn on the floor, surrounded by black tallow candles. He gasped at that sight and was about to leave when her husky voice halted him on his tracks, "Come in, fear not. Me finish."

"I didn't mean to disturb you, just checking if everything's fine," he said.

"Nay. Ju came 'cause ju're attracted t' me, captain," she said, turning slowly and revealing her bare breasts. Drake's irises widened at the sight, due more to the woman's immodesty than the vision of her exposed tits.

"Do not deny it. Me was aware of it by da moment we met. Me have been ridden too many times by *Erzulie Fréda Dahomey* t' know different," she said, coming closer.

Drake felt embarrassment for the first time in his life; he had had his way with many women, yet this time it felt different.

Again, there was some unnatural spell going on here.

"In fact, me was waiting for ju, Drake," she continued, while her hands reached for his shirt and unlaced it.

Drake could not move, transfixed by her beautiful eyes and warmness. He tried to react, by gently pushing her away, but to no avail.

A hot lust overcame his senses and, finally, he surrendered to her bold advances.

Drake skimmed his hands lightly over her breasts, and her peaks reacted, standing out like belaying pins. Heat invaded his soul as he kissed the curve of her neck, and pushed her down on the floor. Embracing her, he pinned her down, cupped a breast, and used his tongue to titillate her nipple. She released a soft moan, then grabbed his hair and drove him further, driving him crazy.

Drums. Slow, but relentless beating filled his ears out of nowhere. A hot waft of air caressed his face as he sensuously slid a finger inside her. She contracted, then relaxed under his passionate action.

The candles in the room flickered to a life of their own, while the drums paired a low rhythm with their movements. Drake burned like fire and ignored all the strange happenings as ardor hurled him high and sent him into a feverish delirium. He lifted his head and as he stared into Kaya's mysterious dark eyes, he knew it was more than coupling—something hard to describe. He wanted more from her, yet what that was, he couldn't say.

After positioning herself, she pulled him inside her. Drake groaned, then grabbed her legs and thrust into her. He seized her *ouanga*—a protective necklace made of chicken bones—and plunged deeply. They started to move like wild animals and the drumming increased its rhythm, turning into a savage tribal symphony. They latched their lips to one another's, taking away their breath, until, finally, both reached climax and the beating pitched into a final thunder.

Lost in her arms, he didn't notice the tiny straw doll—shaped in his image—sitting on the bed.

****

Later, they both lay on the bed, holding each other. Their intercourse had been wild, different from everything Drake had experienced before.

"Why did you do that?" he asked.

She kept her eyes off him, sighed, and then caressed his chest with one hand. "'Cause me needahd it. Dis might be me last act of pure selfishness in dis world."

"What do you mean?" he enquired, concerned.

Kaya rose from the cot and reached for her nightgown, still not daring to look at him. She was tense. "Ju see, da sacrify requires blood. And it will be me blood dat will be spilled into *Mabouya's Well*."

"No! Why do you have to do that? We can find another way. Listen—" he protested, but was interrupted by her stern gaze.

"How much do ju place value on human life, Drake? What's da difference between me life and another's? Me will no take da life of an innocent when me kan stop dis Curse with an offer da Loa kan't refuse."

"I can give 'em another life. I do not want to lose you. Kaya. I'm charmed, I do not know how it happened, but it's true," he continued his protest, but again was shooed by Kaya, this time by her soft lips.

Nevertheless, the argument had to be postponed because the shout from the crow's nest had Drake spring up from bed and reach for his clothes.

"Ship ahoy!"

****

The *Banshee's Cry* rocked gently amid a canyon of rotting husks. Geist had spotted the first of the floating wrecks more than an hour before. Then, they had been engulfed by the mists. Weird sounds echoed in that forlorn landscape made of decaying wood and decomposing floating corpses. The black sea was filled with countless ships in a chaotic cluster. Most of them hung still on the water, but others moved swimmingly around. There were all kinds of ships. From gargantuan Indiamen to tiny sloops. All silent, their sails limping around the masts. And there were the floating bodies. Swollen and moldering, they seemed to drift as if they had been victim of a pirate onslaught or the casualties of battle.

Yet, nobody trusted them to stay that way.

They could rise from one moment to the next, eager to drag the living mariners in their putrid world. The sailors were afraid to utter a single word, as the ship slowly slithered in that endless replica of the Styx.

Once, one of the anchored dead ships seemed to come to life when the brig came too close; the living dead who lay still on the main deck began to rise, scanning with sightless eyes their surroundings. Grinning skulls of bleached bone, empty eye sockets aglow with pale, unholy light, and slack masks of rotting flesh, devoid of human emotion and intelligence. These were the faces of the walking dead: from clattering skeletons come to life to rotting corpses risen from the grave, shambling mindlessly forward, forever hungry. Yet, all returned to their slumber when the *Banshee* changed tack. However, Drake could not shake off the image of one of the monstrosities. A decaying horror encrusted and filled with worms and maggots—that had clearly been a woman—lifted her sickening face from the railings, and stared straight at him. Nevertheless, she saw nothing.

"Dem kan't see we," whispered Kaya into his ear, "Dem kan see only da living's *ti-bon-ange*: da lessah part of da soul dat is tied t' da material world. Dem kan't see da *gros-bon-ange*, dat is da spiritual part, and belongs t' *Bondye*, da Creator."

The sky was turning a dark green-gray color, with dark gray to black clouds rolling above. Wind gusts wafted at the sails from random directions and a chill filled the air. Bluish white bolts of electrical energy shot down from the sky and everything in the area of the coming storm crackled with a halo of unearthly energy.

"Why?" he inquired, worried about that unnatural phenomenon that added dread to an already gloomy landscape.

"Because dem are animated by it. Dem *gros-bon-*

ange remains trapped in da *Well*, instead of traveling beyondah, and since dis lessah force tends t' wane, dem need t' renew it with dat of da living," Kaya explained.

"But why they're not attacking?" he pressed, taking her hand. He was still worried about her purpose.

She looked away, and then added, "Cause of me pact with *Baron Samedi*. Me promised 'im a sacrify at da *Well* and 'im is keeping 'im word. But beware, 'cause *Le Baron* is a trickstah and has a morbid sense of humor." She stopped talking when they entered a tight channel created by two large West Indiaman freighters, their looming hulls towering above the brig like the crumbling walls of a canyon. She signaled to him to stay silent and began murmuring a prayer in Creole.

He understood what the *Baron* considered funny when they spotted the coast of Cayman Brac the following night.

****

After a seemingly endless and silent voyage in the mist-laden sea, Geist was the first to spot land, although he could not cry the usual *'Land Ho!'* signal. It was nightfall and the crew was mostly relaxing below deck, to avoid having their eyes linger too much on hellish surroundings.

Geist rushed down the mizzenmast and caused Mac's heart to falter, believing they were going to crash into one of those hulks.

"We're there, Mac! I spotted the dark outline of an island straight in front of us! I do not know how the hell we did it, blind as we were, but I ensure you, we made it!" he muttered.

"Keep the helm. Me goin' to warn the cap'n," Mac said, then descended the poop deck and knocked on Drake's cabin door.

Drake and Kaya were enjoying their own company when the knocking interrupted their congress. She had lured him even this night, never answering to his pleading requests to abandon her course of action, but keeping his mind occupied with pleasures he had never known.

"What's happening?" Drake peeked out of the cabin.

"Geist just spotted land, Cap'n," Mac said.

"And do you believe..." Drake never finished his question as a chilling scream shattered the quiet. A commotion ensued on the bridge, and Drake's eyes could not distinguish what it was about at first.

Then he saw it.

Luther, the giant, was staggering on the quarterdeck as a disgusting creature chewed at his neck like a hungry dog. The thing comprised of what was left of a sailor's upper body, except that only his decaying head and coiling spine, encased in a coating of algae, remained. The gunner used his strength to get free of the undead vise, but to no use. On the port side, similar creatures and more intact shambling fiends were slowly climbing the railings, while a swollen terror of that cursed sea had already reached the *Banshee*'s deck and was approaching the screaming German.

"Avast! At arms!" Mac cried, while Drake, half-naked, pointed his pistol to the bloated figure and fired. The monster's head exploded like a ripe melon; brainy fluids and splintered bones flew in every direction before he fell overboard. The crew crawled out of the ship's portholes, armed with cutlasses and rifles, yelling battle cries. Drake paused to recharge his pistol, but a hissing sound warned him of the presence of something behind him. This vile creature was outwardly humanoid, with mottled greenish flesh and burning red eyes. Its jaws were large and heavy, and its sick-looking skin sported thorns and spikes. It shambled forward, walking partially on its knuckles like a mighty ape, a nest of slimy tentacle-like growths writhing from its abdomen. If that thing had once been human, it clearly wasn't anymore.

Flintlock expended, Drake went for the cutlass, but the creature was faster. A long black tongue sprang out of its hideous jaws like a moray eel pouncing on a fish, and coiled around his right hand. Immediately it started to reel him in like an angler while lifting its bulging belly from the boards and launching its tentacle-innards toward him. Drake managed to dodge a pair, but a third and a fourth got hold of both his legs and he was whisked toward the abomination at once. Entangled, he tried to hold out his hands to block the incoming bite from the hulking creature, but the fanged maws closed on his right wrist, and he growled in pain as the teeth pierced his flesh.

Abruptly, the creature's skull caved in as a heavy hammer struck it hard just above the brow and fragments of splintered bone flew away, hitting the floor clambering. Then, a blade cut the abomination's prehensile tongue. Black blood sprouted, and what remained of that appendage fell limp on the creature's mouth. Suddenly free, Drake unsheathed his cutlass and jabbed it deep into the undead thing's throat. The beast garbled an eerie protest, but refused to leave its grip on the man's legs. A second blow from the hammer completely destroyed the abomination's skull and a fountain of greenish ooze shrouded its obese body and smeared Drake's face. Finally, the creature abandoned its clasp and an extended hand came into Drake's view.

"Stand up, soldier," Red Leg's terse voice said. Still angry with him, Drake ignored his hand, but nodded a thank you.

A moment later, a group of thin-limbed monstrosities moved behind the Admiral, shambling and limping along in a disheveled pack of eight or nine. Their eyes vacant, skin gaunt and pale, their mouth hung slack, abnormally large and filled with mismatched teeth of different sizes and shapes. Emaciated, almost skeletal beings, these monsters were tall and crooked, with almost transparent skin. Drake saw them approaching the young lad with dark hair who had bravely stood for the crew at *Bluefield's Bay*. He was heroically fighting a group of slouching undead with a barding pike and a gaff.

"Watch out!" he shouted, but it was too late. Bony fingers closed on his shoulders and dragged him down, until he disappeared into the gaunt crowd.

Kaya chose that moment to stick her head out of the cabin. She looked shocked by the sight of those things attacking despite her pact with the Loa. "Tis me fault," she cried..

"Stay inside!" Red Leg shouted, slamming the door shut with a kick and blocking her inside with a heavy barrel.

Shouts and screams rang around them, along with the sound of bursting putrid flesh, as projectiles and blades found their way in the waterlogged raiders. Feeling desperate, Drake moved among the shuffling assailants, slashing with his blade and firing whatever gun came into his hands. But everything was lost. The creatures were swarming out of the water and climbing up from all sides, converging on the living and threatening to sink the very ship with their added mass. The *Banshee's Cry* was doomed.

He watched in horror as Geist was grabbed by a crab-infested and flayed terror, which proceeded to bite his face off, causing blood to flow copiously from the top half of his pale body. Luckily, he died instantly. Drake took his futile revenge by cleaving off the creature's head. Then he went berserk, filled with primal rage as he realized fate and the dead were yanking away all that was left of his personal world. His crew, his friends—his family—and his ship would be gone soon, so he had nothing left to fight for and blindly battled tooth and nail, tearing and crushing, smashing and slashing at the unliving horde. He became a bloodied wolverine: naked and smeared with bodily fluids, bruised and wounded. Nevertheless, he kept going, ignoring pain, and killing as many as he could. His world became sheathed in red and there was only hate.

Yet, there was no end to the unliving horde and soon more warped dead emerged from the depths and climbed up the railings. Muscle and sinew hung from their skeletal bodies while four long, sinewy tendrils writhed from their midsections. Their hollow eye sockets showed nothing and their rotting flesh oozed a vile mixture of blood and mucus. They immediately skittered across the floorboards, pouncing on Charles MacTavish who was frantically trying to dislodge his blade out of the ribs of a skeletal thing encrusted with coral outgrowths that made it look like a humanoid hedgehog. The poor boatswain was soon overwhelmed and opened from crotch to sternum by the horde of crawling monsters, which slithered on their bellies or walked on their hands to reach their prey. The Scotsman fought while he had any strength, kicking and fisting, but soon his screams and curses joined the chorus of the dying.

At the sight of his friend's death, Drake snapped out of his blind fury as a thought crossed his blurred mind: Kaya.

She had been trapped in the cabin by O'Neill, and would probably suffer a similar fate at the hands of those quick things. He imagined them climbing on the hull, reaching the rear windows and crashing inside the quarters. He couldn't allow that to happen.

Drake rushed to the cabin, removed the barrel, and found Kaya holding the crystal skull in her hands. Tiny tendrils of haloed mist poured out of it. He didn't know what she was doing, but there was no time to waste, so he grabbed her by the elbow and hastily shook her off her trance. The crystal skull slipped out of her hands, hit the floor, and rolled under the bed.

"Let's go! The ship's doomed. Your Loa hasn't kept his word," he cried amid the screams of the dying. He ignored the macabre thing clinking under the cot, a yellowish light brightening its depths.

She gave him a hard look, as if angry at him for having interrupted her ceremony. Then her gaze softened as her connection to the material world returned. She nodded, but whispered, "It's not 'im who hasn't kept da promise."

They ran to the lifeboat, forgetful of the skull, while Red Leg continued his stand, killing as many Risen as he could, whilst new horrors continued to climb from the *Banshee*'s starboard. Yet, these weren't Risen, but the dismembered bodies of the Accursed. Somehow, they had got free of the enchantment holding them still, and with renewed vigor began flailing blindly at living and unliving. Even the Crimson Roger's headless body joined battle, the ropes that had held him fastened to the *Banshee*'s bowsprit dangling from his pale frame.

Once the barge was in the water, Kaya and Drake jumped into it, soon reached by Red Leg and two of his goons. "We can still succeed. The island ain't far." He was bloodied and his garish clothes reduced to tattered rags.

Drake barely heard him. He began to row mechanically, oblivious to his surroundings, while Kaya wrapped her hands around his neck. With a sundered heart, Drake uttered a prayer for his lost friends, as he rowed toward the island of the dead.

'*See you soon, my friends,*' he ended his thoughts.

****

Aboard the brig, the mangled body of those who had died began to stir. Their clothes torn and stained with blood, their heads cocking on the side, and vacant eyes, they joined the ranks of the Risen that just took their life and shambled with them. Yet, many stood still, somehow untouched by the Curse as if they were blessed with a final release.

The Crimson Roger's headless body found one of them, almost intact except for his flayed face.

Geist.

He sunk the scythe into the bloodless corpse, and then stood still, looming above it while what was left of his butchered crew systematically kept the Risen horde away from him. Suddenly, the cadaver opened his bloodied eyes and red flames flickered into them. The headless body fell sideways as the new host came to life.

Soon, the thing that once was Geist the Albino strode toward the captain's cabin and knelt to look under the bed.

His pale hand grabbed the crystal skull as a grin creased his skinless face.

CHAPTER THIRTEEN

WHERE BRAVE MEN DO NOT VENTURE

The five survivors paddled amidst a sea of thick rotting matter and festering carcasses. All the water surrounding *Mabouyacay* had been turned into a soupy marsh, buzzing with strange insects whose bloated maggots continually feasted on the decomposing flesh of unrecognizable beings. Some of the corpses had been once human, but were warped beyond recognition, while others looked more like unearthly things, whose natural dwellings were the deep abysses or the nether realms. The stench was unbearable, but there was no way to avoid inhaling it, so they kept retching, yet their empty stomachs could not satisfy that instinctual spasm.

Jetsam jutted out of that green-yellowish tangle, showing the broken mast of a sunken galleon here, the marred figurehead of a long lost bowsprit there. Glass bottles, jugs of evaporated grog, tattered clothes. A rag doll, whose cracked porcelain face had long lost its painted features, gazed at Drake with her lonely glass eye, having him shudder at the fate of the original owner. A grim reminder that the Risen had no mercy to spare on the younger and the infirm. The trip to the shore was terrible and maddening, but they kept rowing as if finally planting their soles on firm land would dissipate all those horrors they were enduring. As soon as they reached the swampy beach, they quickly disembarked, making for a thicket of mangroves to find shelter. In the distance, the cries of dying mariners still played a bloody symphony. The mangrove trees themselves looked warped: their leaves no longer green, but of a putrid yellow, their branches and twisted roots deformed by purulent boils. Stinging gnats buzzed around the men, eager to bite at living flesh.

"We're doomed, Red Leg! I told you it was a foolish deed you were asking from me," Drake said, clenching his teeth, whilst grabbing the older man's ragged shirt. His fury lodged together with the memories of his lost friends. Immediately, the Admiral's goons were on him, but O'Neill stopped them on their tracks.

"We're not doomed, Drake. We're here. Do you see any Risen around, huh? You do not have faith, scurvy dog. That's your fault." He disengaged from Drake's clasp. "But mine's strong and I will not linger here while the end of the Curse is at arm's reach!"

He was as fanatic as the man who had started it all.

Yet he was right. It seemed there were no living dead shuffling around on the beach. For unknown motives, those monsters did not set foot on the island. Drake glanced beyond the older man's shoulders and saw the beach. Empty. No walking dead mulling around. The same was the case inland. No tracks marred the pristine sand up to the jungle's edge. He returned his eyes to Kaya, who was busy tending at his numerous wounds. She poured what was left of the rum jug on his cuts and applied strips of torn fabric.

"Well, ain't goin' to allow this woman's blood sacrifice. Take mine," he proposed, ignoring the disapproving look in Kaya's eyes.

"There's no need to discuss this now, Drake. Let's just get to the cave before it's too late." He detected a condescending note in the elder that made him even more furious.

"No. Ain't comin' unless you reassure me Kaya's life will be spared!" he spat.

"Ju shut up! Both!" Kaya broke in. "Da fact dat dere are no Risen on dis beach mean no worsah horrors kan't be lurking here. We must wait for dawn. Dem dead move only undah dark; light is dem enemy and dem spend da day by lying still till da sun goes down." She tightened a strip of cloth at Drake's bicep. "We must find shelter. Me'll protect it with a spirit ward. We kan't stay in da open."

Red Leg nodded, keeping his stare on Drake. "Right. I'll send me boys to find a cave or whatever will suit us." The two fighters exchanged a worried look, but said nothing.

Then, the heavy thumping of something large moving among the mangroves caught their attention and all heads turned to the direction of the sound. Quickly, they squatted, lying as low as they could. Kaya lifted one finger to her lips for them to be quiet. The thumping repeated, then paused, then repeated, then paused again. Those were steps from something huge. Kaya gripped her *ouanga* and silently uttered a prayer to *Ghede*.

Soon, something hard to discern entered their vision. More than nine feet tall, the flesh of this being was dotted with rotting pustules and a gagging reek wafted from it like meat gone bad. Writhing pockets of white maggots were visible in some of the open sores upon its body. It had two strong, tree trunk-like legs whose feet looked like the stumps of an amputee. Powerful arms—warped, but threateningly effective—jutted at the sides of a composite mass of dead bodies melted together to form a sturdy torso. Naked, the creature had no visible sex, yet many of the orifices and protuberances (set at odd places) on its flesh resembled female and male genitalia. It had no head as such, just a cavernous hole where the neck was supposed to be, and inside its depths splintered and jagged bones, glistening, stuck out of the dead meat in the imitation of a lamprey's mouth. The thing moved with an uneven gait and every step seemed to cause it pain, as every time one of the 'feet' touched the ground a low gurgle escaped from the mouth-like orifice.

Luckily, the thing crossed the patch of mangroves, ignoring them.

As soon as the abomination left their field of vision, one of O'Neill's men was overcome by panic and, screaming like a five year old, he crashed into the vegetation on the opposite direction.

"Stop him!" Red Leg ordered the other fighter. "He's gonna call that thing back!"

Merciless, the goon aimed his flintlock rifle at the frightened comrade, but Drake hastily grabbed the weapon's muzzle. "Are you crazy? This gonna attract unwanted attention to us!" The soldier trained a baleful gaze at him, but then relaxed. Drake kept his hand on the rifle. "Besides, he'll surely cause a commotion. Thar be Risen hiding around, we'll soon find out."

He was right. As soon as the screaming mariner reached the open, a pair of dried hands erupted from the grit, grasped the running man's feet, and sent him flying out of his boots, down to bite the sand. Immediately, more hands exploded from the ground and started to drag him below. The sailor flailed and kicked desperately, but could not fight off all those claws and soon they dug into his flesh with bony fingers, spearing him like a whale, and pulling and tearing from opposite directions. His shrills attracted the towering monster back, and the creature crossed the thicket with unexpected speed, extended one of its long arms and closed its steely fingers on the poor man's head. Then, like a kid playing with a doll, tore off the upper part of the body from the craving hands, forcibly separating it from the abdomen and legs. For a moment, the man's entrails distended rigidly like strings on a cello, until they snapped, raining their bloody content on the wavering hands. The monster lifted what was left of the screaming man to its 'mouth', then tucked the thrashing morsel into it and the hole closed with a disgusting munching sound.

"Well, the beach ain't safe," Drake mouthed. "And me don't reckon the jungle as safe as well."

"Ju're wrong," said Kaya, who had turned her eyes from the ghastly scene. She was looking at something within the bog. "Dere's a hut ovah dere."

O'Neill and Drake followed her gaze. She was right, for partly hidden by the warped trees, stood a decrepit, yet still intact, primitive structure. It rose out of the marshy waters, deep inside the mangrove thicket, like a gnarled tree stump. Draped by Spanish moss, short but effective stilts supported the house, keeping it out of the water.

"Even if somethin' inhabits it," she whispered, "we kan kill it. Then we kan make a *humfor* outta it. Me'll draw a *verver* at da entrance, so t' confuse da dead."

O'Neill detected Drake's befuddled look. "A *verver* is a sacred design drawn at the doorway of a voodoo worship place. Its lines and whorls bar the way to *baka* and *djab*—evil spirits—by forcing them to follow the pattern of circles. They become lost forever in the design. Risen are in effect ridden by these creatures, so they will stay away from the *verver*." He turned to Kaya. "Do you still have your *gris-gris*?"

"No. Me lost it, but me kan use jurs." She pointed at a small drawstring bag hanging at Red Leg's neck. "Hand it t' me."

The Admiral removed the leather necklace and turned it over to her. Drake smirked. "How long have ya been into this, Morgan?"

"By a long time. You can't imagine." The girl opened the satchel and a smell of strange herbs wafted out. Inside, Drake could see that there was indeed a mixture of dried leaves and what looked like tiny strips of cloth. Noticing his curiosity, the elder man explained. "Half of these herbs and bundles of fabric have been mounted by bad spirits. The other half by good ones. They create a magical empowerment for the Mambo or *Houngan* performing a ceremony. The opposite spirits fighting each other generate power to be used in a spell."

Drake spotted the hulking monster slowly coming back to the thicket. "Aye *amigos*, whatever ya have in mind better do it fast, because that thing," he pointed to the rotting giant, "just finished its snack and is longing for more."

Quickly, but stealthily, they moved toward the

hut.

****

Silent, they climbed the broken ladder up to the tiny landing. The place was crumbling, but its door still held up on its hinges. There was no sign of inhabitation, yet the four from the *Banshee* stood alert, their weapons ready to strike. Under the porch dangled dozens of charms and wardings of the voodoo faith, yet Kaya immediately understood that this hadn't been the *humfor* of a Mambo, but the dark abode of a *Bokor*, a conjure doctor.

Red Leg signaled for his bodyguard to open the door, but Drake—who had retrieved some emergency items from the boat—stopped him in his tracks. He fished a lantern from the small sack he was carrying, lit it, and handed it to the man. "I'll open the door. You just brighten it."

The large goon gladly accepted his role and positioned himself. Drake went over to push the door ajar, but before he could do that, Kaya grabbed his elbow. "Be wary. Me feel a presence here," she whispered.

He nodded, then slowly pushed the door in. The hut was dark and empty. They stared for a while, adjusting their tired eyes to the light before noticing something moving up ahead in the pitch black, just at the edge of the lantern's beam.

"Look. Look upon t' ground," Kaya said in a

hushed whisper.

All along the floorboards were drawings of children. Children jumping, children playing, children as they must have been in their daily lives. Strangely, all of the scrawled figures had blank faces. No one had any eyes or mouth. Just an empty circle where a face should have been. Drake gazed upon the drawings, which extended away into the darkness.

A scuffling noise ahead caught their attention. Startled, Red Leg tore the lantern from his man's grip and stepped forward, holding it high.

There, dancing in the darkness of the hut, were two little girls. Their once white dresses were now stained with mud and dried blood. One of them paused and turned toward the intruders, while the other kept twirling on her tiptoes. Though she faced them, her features were hidden by her dark hair, which lay haggard over her gray face like a shroud of kelp and seaweeds. "D'ju wanna come n' play?" she asked with a voice that sounded disjointed and older than her age.

The other glanced in same direction, still gyrating, and gave a giggle, her face hidden by her hand, which she used to courteously hide her mocking laughter in the way of well mannered noble kids.

Suddenly, a terrible stench rode the air—the smell of rot and decay pressed over the place like a smothering hand. There could be no doubt about the fate of those poor little girls. They were Risen.

"Come n' play," the first one repeated.

Surprised by the voice, O'Neill stepped back, but Kaya grabbed his arm. "Do not bade away," she said. "Dis is what ju have come for."

He turned toward her. "We came here looking for the *djab*," he said. "Not these two abominations."

The little girl, whose face lay covered by her long, bedraggled hair, made a step forward. "Me am *djab*. Yet, Me also am Kehinde, da Voodoo Queen." Her voice grated like a scratched harpsichord.

Aghast, frozen in place, as if his blood had turned stiff and still like a winter-born stream, O'Neill spoke again but with great effort—"I have come seeking *Mabouya*. I come on behalf of *Baron Samedi*. This horse," he pointed to Kaya, "is here for the sacrifice."

Drake stepped in, much to the contempt of Red Leg and Kaya. "Take me."

The undead girl released a giggle through her hairy shroud. "Well," said the other girl, stopping her cavorts. "Ju came t' da righ' place. We are *Mabouya*. But we want no sacrify."

Holding each other's hand, the bodies of the two girls stepped into the light. In the dimness of the lantern, upon the floor drawn with the perverse mockery of children's drawings, the two of them revealed their hideous features, their half-eaten visages. Skull-like faces grinned under curtains of unnaturally lush raven black hair.

When they spoke, they spoke as one.

"Tell *le Baron* we want no sacrify. We got everythin' we want." Their eye sockets were empty, but the thing—or the woman—who filled their bodies like they were gloves, could see them. "Ju might be curious t' know why me kan speak from two bodies at once, don't ju?"

"Me know jur story, Kehinde. Me know what happened t' jur people. Me know jur pain. But da world ju created kan't go on like dat. Soon, it will be only ju n' nothing else," said Kaya.

The twins ignored her. "It is 'cause me am both of dese bodies. Me am in many places at once. Me am *Mabouya* now. Each person me collect becomes part of me, and me have collected many people. Me have ridden da youngah and da ole, da healthy n' da sick. And now, me will ride j'all."

"And then there'll be none," intruded Drake. "What for? You grab all the toys, then there's no one to play with. It's just like playin' dices by yourself. You always win."

"Perhaps." The twins advanced slowly, their heads turned to him, hands still linked. "But me am no da only one in dis playground. Sometimes, da dead come back. Sometimes dem come back 'cause dem are cursahd; otha times, dem come back 'cause someone did no bury dem properly. Then, dere are dose havin' unfinishad business t' complete. Dem are me playmates in dis Deadworld. Ju are just toyz."

"What about the Loa?" Drake pressed, gripping

his hand on the cutlass.

"Da Obedient, or da Risen as ju call me, toyz, do no return for any of dese reasons," the twins continued. "Dem return 'cause me has wrenched dem from da earth with *magie*, lockin' dem back into dem dead bodies. When dis happens, they kan only watch as dem are paraded around like puppets. Cause dat's what dem are—puppets." They pirouetted, then returned to place, with the grace of theater dancers. "Like all puppets, dem must have someone pulling da strings. Ju had your kings and queens doin' dat for centuries. Dem used ju as pawns in all dem wars. What's changed? Nuthin', me tell ju."

"I serve no one," Drake spat, advancing. "But you are still a puppet, Kehinde. You are just a puppet for the thing inside you. Slave you were born and still a slave you are. I know it hurts, but you can't deny that. Do you feel it, Kehinde? Do you feel it within you? You are fighting its war, not yours."

The twins cocked their head as if they were pondering, then pulled up their lips in a ghastly smile. "*Oui*. Dis is a war. But it's me war. And me have relentless soljers. A livin' soljer must eat. He must sleep. He needs money n' sheltah. Even with such things provided t' 'im, a soljer kan still betray ju. A walking body, though, has no need for dese things. It only needs someone t' pull da strings. It doesn't betray ju. Ju kan order it to kill children and it will do. No hesitashun."

"But you are just feeding the *djab*, Kehinde. It needs them *gros bon ange*, nothing else." He was just at arm's reach now. "You said it. The Obedient are just toys. No one cares if they lose a few puppets. New ones can always be made. And you will be dismissed when *Mabouya* will find a better one."

He swung his cutlass in a wide arc hoping to chop both heads in a strike. But his hand was blocked in midair by a strong, unexpected grip. Drake turned to face the unseen adversary who was protecting his puppeteer. And, with horror, he found it was Red Leg.

Morgan O'Neill's eyes had rolled up, showing the white. A deathly grin marred his already scarred features and drool oozed out of his mouth like foam from a raging dog.

The twins released a chilling laugh. "D'ju wanna know da worst way ju can use da puppets, mariner?"

Drake struggled to get free, but he ceased when more hands blocked his movements. The goon had been taken, too.

"T' strike terror 'n fear in da hearts of da innocent. When me use ju dis way, me wanna inflict emotional damage. Cause jur essence doubles n' gets tastier. Fear is da most sweet of cakes, cap'n."

Desperate, Drake turned to Kaya. But she was nowhere to be seen.

"Me kan use my toyz t' taunt me victims. By

night, dere may be strange footsteps about jur door, accompanied by da sound of clicking bones n' rustling chainz. Dere might be scraping at da window." They came closer while talking.

Drake's cutlass was wrestled from his hand and it clacked on the floor. He was pushed down by the ridden men and forced to stand at the girls' level.

"Da most horrify deed me kan do, of course, is t' get da bodies of dose me victim knows. Me have done dis many times, riding da loved ones of me victims one by one. Ju kan't imagine dem taste." The twins lunged forward, ready to bite his face off. But stopped just inches away. "D'ju know jur worst sin, Drake?"

Having lost everything, Drake was not afraid to die. To hell with the world. He just wished to die for real, his soul lost to oblivion. Surprisingly, his last thought ran to Lorraine Dumont, not to Kaya.

He grinned, ready to die. "Aw. I love all seven."

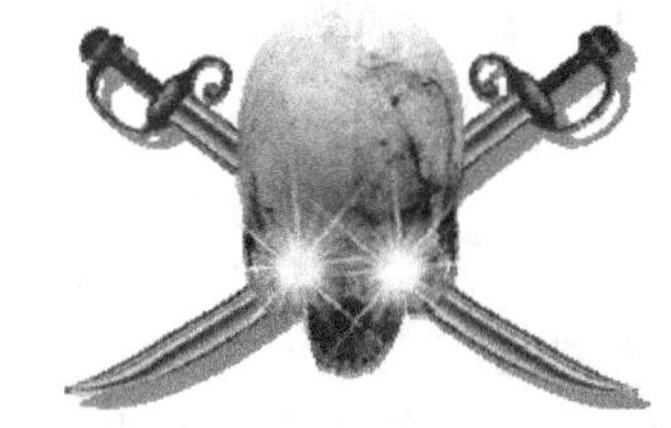

CHAPTER FOURTEEN

WELL OF SOULS

Drake stared into the eyes of the twins as they got closer, eager to sink their gnashing teeth into his face. The thing occupying their bodies, the thing that once had been a woman but was now a monster, savored every instant craving his fear. Nonetheless, Daniel was too angry, he had been witness to too much horrors, and having lost everything he was anchored with, he felt nothing. He wasn't afraid to die. He almost wished for it to end his suffering. So, the twins recoiled and a mask of disappointment creased their revolting faces.

"Aren't ju 'fraid t' die?"

"No, sorry for not being as tasty as you expected." He didn't take off his gaze from their empty sockets. He didn't know how, but he would do everything to bring that creature down to Hell with him. He tried to focus, but his thoughts kept running to Lorraine. Her blue gems sparkled into the dark recesses of his mind; he felt a rush of blood in his heart and in his empty stomach, butterflies took flight.

"Me am gonna last her longah. Me will no kill her fast," gloated the evil chorus in triumph. The queen had peered into his mind and heart, finding what he cared for. "And me will wear jur body when me will do that!" They both cackled.

At that, an unnatural strength took possession of his body, and he pulled free of his captors, viciously headbutted both twins, quickly stood and punched Red Leg in the nose. The Admiral's bodyguard was on him before he could find a way to defend, battering him with a series of hammer blows. He staggered back into the dark and saw both ridden men coming for him. Desperately, he scanned his bare surroundings to find a weapon, but there were none. Even his cutlass was nowhere to be seen. Except...

He spotted the skeletal remains of something long beyond reanimation: a bunch of jagged bones and a cracked skull. Another kid. He grasped a fragmented femur.

The possessed goon rushed toward him, hands extended, trying for his neck, but he hastily blocked him, and with a swift move, sunk the bone right into the man's left eye. The tip of the weapon impaled through the socket and smashed up, through the top of the man's skull, impaling his brain and leaving his body hanging, deadweight, on the weapon. One down.

Red Leg extracted his flintlock and trained it at him.

Everything happened so fast that Drake didn't at first grasp what came about.

He saw the Admiral pointing the gun at him, and the twins behind him, holding hands. Then, a shadow moved rapidly in, hiding them from his vision. He saw Kaya—for the shadow was Kaya—bend down and blow off a gray powder off her palm. O'Neill cocked the pistol, ready to fire, while the two girls screamed in rage as the powder clung to their faces. Then, before the controlled Admiral could fire, the black woman pummeled him on the back of his head with Drake's cutlass, twirled on herself, and slashed the blade across both undead girls' necks. Their heads fell, but their bodies stood there, still holding hands. At the same time, Red Leg crumbled down to the floor; his pistol escaped his grip and disappeared in the dark.

Finally, exhausted, Drake let his legs stop holding him up and he collapsed against the wall. Kaya came into his view, her beautiful dark eyes shining in the dim light.

"It's no ovah yet," she said. "We must still go to t' well." She smiled seeing that Drake was safe. He tried a grin, but his strength failed him.

"Yet, ju must rest before dat. Sleep, Drake. Me will make this place safe." Those were the last words he heard before falling into a dreamless slumber.

****

No creature disturbed their hiding place that night, and when Drake woke up, he saw Kaya peeking out of the door. She seemed worried.

The sun was struggling to brighten the island through the thick cluster of dark clouds perennially covering the cursed land. Its feeble rays shone through the cracks in the hut's boards, but were not powerful enough to entirely light it up.

Drake noticed a movement to his left and quickly reached for his gun. But he had none.

"Rise n' shine soldier," Red Leg said as he washed the dried blood off his face by pouring some of the water from his flask and rubbing vigorously. From his position, Drake made out the big lump at the back of his head where Kaya had hit him so hard that he had lost his senses. "We're almost over. Kaya has banished the Queen to the well, but tonight she will take possession of a new body. So, we must perform the ceremony before sundown."

"It's not just dat," Kaya said, without taking her eyes off whatever she was spying. "We must act quickly or dis place will kill we. Dere's an aura here, some kinda drainin' effect. Da livin' are sapped by it. Within an hour or maybe three, we will be dead. Da well itself leeches da life out of whoever sets foot on da island in daylight. Only da dead kan linger here."

"So why we waited for sunup?" Drake lifted his body from the floor. His muscles ached everywhere. Even his bum hole.

"'Cause me did no know afore," she said bluntly.

****

They began their trek to *Mabouya's Well* under the feeble morning light. First, they passed by the stumps of a burned native village, decorated with blackened bones and charred hides. Then, they reached the cave, the shape of which reminded Drake of a natural-carved skull.

Inside, in total darkness, stood a large oval-shaped hole, some kind of pit, yet no human hand had dug it. The stench of death and offal coming from it was so strong that Drake and Red Leg couldn't avoid throwing out what was left of their meager breakfast of berries that Kaya had judged safe to eat. Yet, she seemed unhindered by it.

"Please, stand back," she said, but her voice was cold, different from the one Drake had started to love.

"Aye," Red Leg said, immediately grabbing Drake by the shoulders to avoid any interference in the Mambo's ritual. She was rapidly drawing weird twirls and symbols all around the hole.

"I can't allow her…" he pleaded. He had to stop her, but felt his life waning away. Kaya was right: soon they would be dead.

"No, Drake. Listen to me. Come over here and wait. There's no other way," O'Neill insisted.

Drake's energy was leaving him, yet he still fought for Kaya's life. She was the last thing he held dear.

"She must do what must be done, Drake. And do not worry, we aren't going to survive all of this," Red Leg said calmly. He was fatigued, too; his icy eyes faded and reddened. "Yes, we're doomed, but mankind's not. Our descendants will live in a better world, freed from the horrors of our age."

Kaya began to chant and whirl on herself, her athletic body moving sinuously in rhythm with her words.

"I love her; I don't care about the rest of the world. I want her!" Drake protested.

Then, darkness engulfed him.

NOW

1708 AD

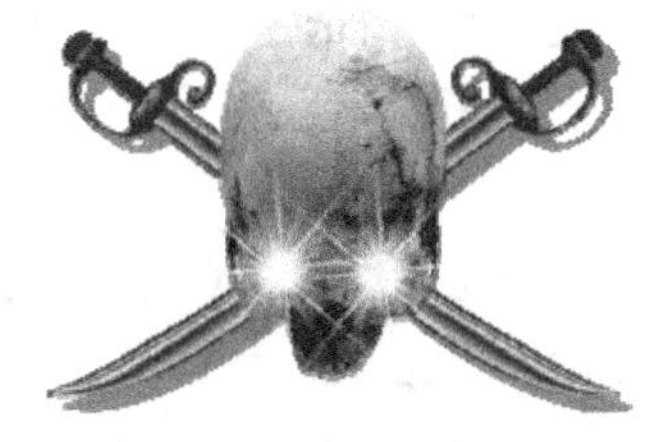

CHAPTER FIFTEEN

THE CHEST

Port Royal, Jamaica

"What happened, then?" prompted Higgins, the young sailor, when Captain Daniel Drake ended his tale. The story had been fascinating and all those details had piqued his curiosity. Yes, he was still convinced that was just tavern talk, but a part of truth had to be there.

"What happened?" repeated the old man, "This world happened. The one you live in. No shambling dead, no Plague. No Curse." He lifted his boots from the table and recovered his leather tri-corn hat. His dark hair had a grizzled shine at the sides, but the man was still strong and somewhat handsome.

The *Black Gull* was empty now. Most of the rowdy customers had left, filling the brothels or dozing off the booze in the streets.

"But what about Kaya? Did she really kill herself?" Higgins asked, sincerely curious.

Drake eyed him, then finished his drink and

rose from his stool. "It's late, bucko. We leave early on the morrow, better for ya to git some sleep," he said, grinning. His face bore a thousand scars.

"No," Higgins protested, "you promised me the proof of your statements, sir," He had to show this 'proof' to gain his respect.

Drake bent his aching back to the chest and opened it. At that, the boy's eyes widened in disbelief at the sight of what lay inside the box.

"See. Ain't telling no tall tales, lad," Drake said gravely.

Higgins officer staggered backward to get some distance from the thing, which twitched and quivered inside the container.

"After the island of the dead made me senseless, Kaya sacrificed Red Leg's life to *Mabouya*. This lifted the Curse, and caused all the dead to return to them graves. Alas, since me gal decided to cheat on *le Baron*, he resolved to cheat back on her. Ya see, the *Baron* had asked for her to remain pure, but she'd offered me her virtue. Her sacrifice would be worthless. Kaya understood this when the Risen had attacked the *Banshee* despite her protections. So, she had opted to sacrifice her innocence by committing murder."

"Where's she now?" the boy asked, still gazing at the now closed chest.

"Dead. She's been killed one month ago, along with me kids."

"How?"

"This was part of the *Baron*'s joke." He stood, straightened his back, farted, and then propped the hat on his head. "Red Leg returned from the grave and joined the *Marauders* on the *Banshee's Cry*. His ship is the last of the living dead unto this world. The *Black Brig* still sails the oceans, me laddie, continuing the Plague's legacy. Yet, it's no longer able to spread it. It only feeds on butchered pain. That's why they whisk away people."

"Who's that arm from?" demanded the youngster, still shocked.

Drake gave him a sad gold and silver smile. "After he killed Kaya and me daughters, that was the only thing I've found of him. He left it on purpose. To let me find him. You see, young lad, tomorrow we will depart to hunt down the Black Brig. And you, bucko, you're goin' to be my First Mate."

Inside the chest, Red Leg's severed arm twitched in anticipation.

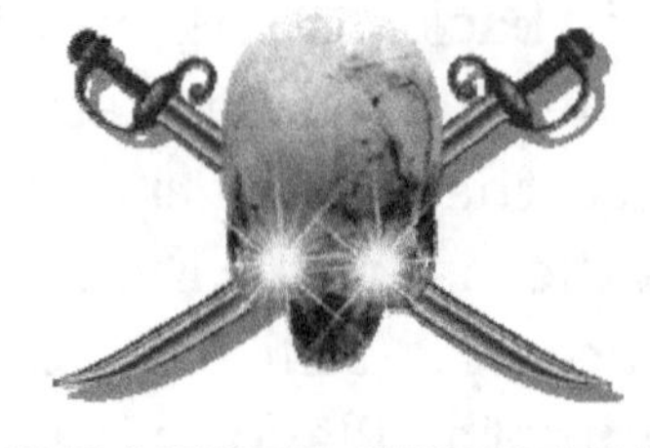

CHAPTER SIXTEEN

THE REVENGE

Port Royal, Jamaica

Captain Daniel 'Drake' Davies stood with one foot propped on the prow's gunwale, his muscled arms folded behind his back, waiting as the waking sun painted the horizon in shades of pink and orange. The wind picked up, tussling Drake's curly black hair, now spattered with white streaks. His steel-gray eyes—once bright and lively, but now dulled and hardened by too many horrors—scanned the horizon while the crew of the *Revenge* readied the ship for departure from Port Royal. Looking at Drake, one got the impression of a suppressed fury, like he was at war with God himself. And in fact, he was. Around his neck, all the necklaces of his past memories were gone, now replaced by a single leather cord, from which hung an ugly gray-green stone charm.

Robert J. Higgins looked at him from under the shadow of the great battleship. The *Revenge* was an imposing vessel, terrifyingly beautiful and beaming out power. Fully rigged, bristling with forty cannons and with a strong profile, she sported a pretty figurehead depicting a comely female in pirate garb.

"Cap'n, she's ready to set sails whene'er you are," a stout, but grizzled quartermaster called from behind him. He didn't turn, but kept his stare down on the young officer. A sad smile cracked his face.

"Get ready to hoist anchor, Norbert," he said, then mostly to himself. "Though, honestly, I'm not so eager to leave." He clutched the small idol in his fist, then strode to meet the young officer onboard.

Higgins straightened in a military salute. He was in full League Militia garb, his red coat spotless and ironed. "I ask permission to come aboard, captain."

Drake valued him with a grin. Hell, this was still a private ship, not a floating circus of the Antillean Navy. "Permission granted. Welcome aboard the *Revenge*, laddie." He caught sight of some of his men smirking and sniggering at the lad's foppish clothes. They were all seadogs, seasoned and grown out of the regular navy. "Bucko," he jeered, "do me a favor. Get down to the outfitter ... and wear somethin' more suitable for this Lady of the sea."

Higgins looked at him, perplexed. "I wear the insignia of our fleet. I'm a liaison officer and—"

"Wanna be my First Mate, laddie?" Drake

interrupted. "Take off that stuff. We ain't goin' to bring battle to the Marauders with you dressed like that." Quickly, he snatched one of his coattails. "These are grips for them claws. Finery like that is good at court or parading down High Street. We aren't going impressing ladies, but facing the worst horrors you have ever seen."

With that, he turned toward the quartermaster. "Hoist sails, Norbert. Ahead full. Let's get this thing done." Adjusting his tri-corn hat on his head, he got over the prow, grabbing a line from the spritsail.

"Raise anchor! Hoist sail! Smartly now, heave to!" the quartermaster immediately began barking orders as he moved back toward the rear of the ship. The crew began to move quickly and efficiently along the deck and rigging, and the tall ship slid through the water toward her future.

****

Drake couldn't sleep that night. He had that odd sense something was wrong, but still couldn't figure it out. So, he strode onto the main deck and a light breeze wafted on his worn face. The sea was calm and there was excellent visibility. Higgins was leaning on the rails, immersed in his thoughts.

"Why aren't you sleeping, lad?" he queried. "Worried? Or you just miss your fancy uniform?" The young officer was wearing now the simple clothes all privateers and common sailors wore on private ships—knee-length breeches and a plain shirt—and stood barefooted on the wooden planks.

"We're heading down the Leeward Chain, aren't we?" Higgins pointed to port. The low, dark profile of Hispaniola appeared in the distance. Drake nodded, then reached for his hipflask and took a swig. He wiped his lips and passed the grog to the officer, but he shook his head. "No, thanks. I never drink alcohol on duty, sir."

Drake smirked. "As you wish, bucko." He gulped down another shot. "Aye, we're heading for Crab, a tiny rock in the Virgin Islands. The trap will be set up there."

"How can you be sure the Black Brig will show up? There's no way to predict where that infamous ship will strike. The Marauders could be everywhere." He paused, then, shook his head. "Guess you have a sorcerous way." He was probably remembering the living arm inside the chest.

"Aye, kiddo." Drake palmed the ugly idol in his palm. "After my escape from *Mabouyacay*, I visited many *bokors* and *houngans*. I learned them ways … and those of the dead."

Higgins changed subject abruptly. "Did you marry Kaya?"

Drake stared in the distance. "No. You see, lad, after I nearly lost my life in that cursed place, I discovered I didn't love her. She had just used me for her own plans. Kaya had cast a spell on me just to appease *Ghede*. The Lord of the Dead had told her in a ceremonial mounting that she had to bear child for him. Somehow, I was the chosen one, the one *Ghede* would mount to give her the daughters he needed. So, she used a spell to enthrall me, to bend me to her will. But in the end, my true love for another woman won over, and I confronted her with it."

The young sailor looked at him quizzically. "I do not understand, sir. She had to stay pure for the *Baron*, but the other entity wanted her to bear progeny?"

"Aye. The Loa are unpredictable and hard to understand. *Ghede* had his plans. And *Baron Samedi* his own. The various spirits often clash, like the ancient gods of Greece. Maybe, they are the same things that haunted Hercules or Achilles. Who knows?' He moved toward the prow to have a better look at the open sea. "When I woke up in the cave, Kaya's hands were red with blood. She had killed Red Leg and sent his body down the well. I expected myself to be happy, because she didn't sacrifice herself. Yet, I just felt anger. I was angry with her and couldn't feel the same passion that had burned inside me." He passed a hand over his eyes, as though that would send away the memories, but it didn't help. "She was different. Unsmiling. A true bride of *Ghede*, not the woman I loved. The curse was over, but I sensed we had just done something worse. We had traded one disease for another. So, I confronted her, angrily. And she told me everything about the tiny voodoo doll and how she had enthralled me."

"How did you escape from the cay?"

"My wife. She helped me." Drake smiled.

"Your wife?"

"Well, she wasn't my wife in those times, but I married her shortly thereafter. Lorraine had followed us to the island. And when she came ashore, she found Kaya and me. We got back to Jamaica aboard the *Raven's Nest*, but not before leaving Kaya in Tortuga."

"You said your relationship couldn't work—"

"Aye. But things like that can change a man's soul. After defeating the Curse, I left the account, married the woman I really loved, and settled down my own trading company. I used to freight cargo in all the Caribbean, and to friendly ports. But I knew in my heart it wouldn't last. I knew this thing would haunt me for years, so when the first tales about the Marauders reached my ears, I knew I had a place in this." Drake turned and walked toward his cabin. "Lad, listen to me. Forget about everything. Forget about duty, honor, and the old ways. This is a different world. In this place, women and men must fight side by side. There's no more space for chivalry, for our nights are full of the horrors we have unleashed. And we need all able hands. The Good Lord has abandoned us. We are just fanciful puppets in the hands of capricious gods."

"Where's she now? Your wife, I mean?" Higgins followed him close.

Drake opened the cabin's door, and then turned. "Oh, she never changed, lad. She still commands a crew and goes her own way. She's like the sea. And you can't tell the sea to be calm or be rough. It has its own mind." He winked. "You'll see her soon. The original *Raven's Nest* went down the waves back in '81. She's got more ships, after that. Stronger, sturdier, an' bigger. But she christened all of 'em with the same name: the *Raven's Nest.*"

"Good night, captain." Higgins bowed curtly.

Drake looked at him. "Oi, kiddo," he smiled through gold and silver. "Don't piss the lady off, tomorrow."

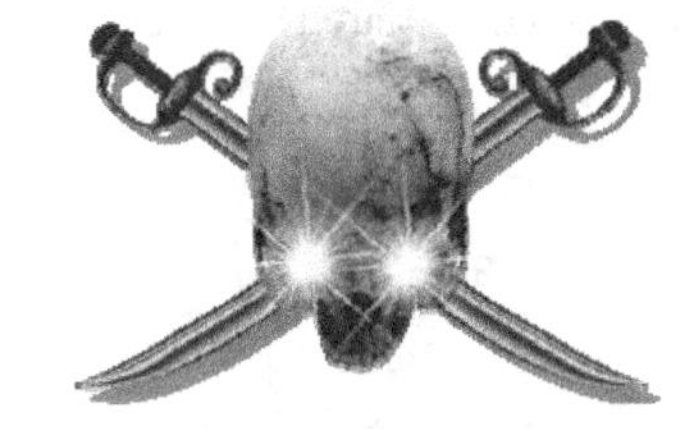

CHAPTER SEVENTEEN

THE BLACK BRIG

In the early morning hours, the *Revenge* reached the inner lagoon of the abandoned colony of Crab Island, just outside the swampy waters of Coffin Bay, and Captain Drake gave orders to drop anchor. Drake and Higgins stood by the ship's railings, looking across the tight channel leading to the pristine lagoon. There was something hostile and haunting about Crab Island. The land appeared scrubby, with low sawgrass and gnarled mangroves. The very air was humid and hot to breathe and carried a bad smell. Memories of *Mabouyacay* swept inside Dan's mind like an ill wind.

"Yes, this is the place," he said, while fisting the idol in his right hand. "They are here, hiding from the light, and waiting for darkness to come."

The young mariner looked at him. "Where are they hiding? I can't see anything."

Drake smirked. "The *Black Brig* is anchored just off the coast of Butcher's Bay." He pointed eastward. "She stands there, popping like a cork in the waters, her decks empty, but truly … a floating tomb of cannibal monsters."

He handed Higgins the spyglass, knowing he'd see the monstrous brig dancing on the waves in a secluded bay. It was all black, except for the yellow-white bones adorning her hull. The black sails stood limp on burned masts, painted with red symbols. A necklace of severed heads stood nailed on the prow's rim, like obscene hunting trophies of a cannibalistic tribe. Nothing moved on her decks and even the birds seemed to avoid it. "Are we going to blast that thing to Heaven, sir?"

Drake moved to the aft castle. "Aye. That's your duty, along with my spouse's." He pointed to the south. There, the silhouette of a large West Indiaman, with stark white sails, loomed on the horizon. "That's her ship, the *Raven's Nest*. You are going to command the *Revenge* in this battle, lad, not me." Then, he climbed the stairs to the helm, where an old sea artist was placing moorings at the large wheel.

Higgins rushed after him. "What are you saying, sir? With all due respect, I'm not ready to lead men to battle. What are you going to do?"

Drake ignored him and stood tall on the castle, addressing the crew. "From this moment, I leave command of this ship to Mister Robert J. Higgins, late of Jamestown. I want eight of the most battle-hardened men. Men who know and trust me. Men whose heart bleeds with rage toward those things. I know many of you enrolled on my ship just to bring your revenge on these devils. Well, lads, that day has come. We are going to end this once and for all."

One of the crewmembers stood. "Captain, what about the booty? These monsters have plundered villages and ports for years."

"There's no booty, lad," Drake smiled sadly, "but our reward is greater than any treasure. Our prize is revenge, nothing else. Any man who sees the danger as too much will be put ashore, in this bay, and I will respect his decision. I will not look down on him." He made a pause. No one stepped forward. "*Bueno*," he continued. "I'm going to send the captain of the *Black Brig* to Hell. I need eight brave volunteers to follow me in this battle of faith." He showed the crew the idol. "This gris-gris was gifted to me by *Baron Samedi* himself. The guardian of the dead has promised his help in this fight. He said he never allowed this monstrosity to be made and he won't allow it to go on. A precious servant of *Ghede* has been butchered recently, along with her daughters who were meant to bring renewal in this blasted world. The captain who leads the Marauders is not acting under the will of the Loa, but is just carrying on a legacy of the past. We have the favors of the Loa."

At this, there was an enormous uproar among the crew, as they were all followers of the faith. Several minutes passed before Drake was able to get them silent again. "Eight brave men. I just need eight!" he shouted.

Eight burly and scarred fighters stepped forward, the glint of rage in their eyes.

"Are you with me?" Drake shouted again. "Are you ready to bring revenge?"

The whole crew responded as one.

****

Drake took eight of his men onto the island and deep into the sparse jungle. They knew that they might not survive the fight, yet all would follow the will of the Loa. They crouched and peered out into a clearing. It was then that he heard the first of the cannon fire and hoped that both the *Revenge*—and mostly his spouse's ship—would be thorough in destruction. The *Black Brig* had to be swept away before sundown. And the thought of his old brig being sunk down to Davey Jones hurt him.

In the clearing, Drake saw a large hole set in the middle, going down below the ground, and large enough to let pass crouching men. Above the hole, a churning, roiling smoke rose into the sky, swirling out to become the fog that would shroud the cursed ship by night.

Drake and his men braved the mists and slowly descended into the rocky hole. They were nervous, but resolute. No faltering now. The Marauders' captain and his bodyguards were surely slouching in the dark, waiting for the moon to replace the sun high in the sky. They couldn't sleep, they couldn't die, but they could be defeated.

Suddenly, Drake spotted a figure holding a crystal skull in one hand and a knife in the other. It stood over a body, removing the dead man's skin. The figure wore the red clothes of the Crimson Roger, yet his features were those of someone he knew. Someone he had cared for.

Geist.

The figure stopped working and gazed across the cave. The Crimson Roger's laughing voice wheezed out of his throat. "Drake, old friend! We were wondering when you'd find this place. Since our last meeting, we've been rather anxious to add your soul to our crew." Geist's gaunt and pale face looked even more ghastly now, with a deathly grin frozen on his lips.

The interior of the cave was larger than Drake expected. Inside the wide underground grotto, four figures shambled, dragging their feet on the stony ground. They were all patched up, with skins of different colors sewn directly on their bones. Fishhook piercings, disgusting holes, and burned wounds marred their dead flesh, while their dull eyes turned on the him and his men with murderous intent. All were naked, except the Crimson Roger.

Drake was stunned by the sight of his old friend's body, now being used as a garment by the unholy soul. He spotted a dark figure shambling forward. The body missed an arm.

Admiral Morgan 'Red Leg' O'Neill shuffled toward him with empty eyes. Naked, his pale flesh scarred and stitched together, what was once one of the most powerful men in the League's fleet was now just a thrall under the command of the Crimson Roger. He'd despised Red Leg, yet he felt pity for him. So ambitious, so selfish, he had fallen in the trap of faith.

The Crimson Roger moved closer too and tilted his head. "Can you hear that?" A rumbling sound echoed from outside the cave. "Those are the cannons of the *Banshee's Cry* turning your ship into nothing but flotsam."

"You are wrong, Braziliano," Drake scoffed, "those belong to the *Raven's Nest*. She dug a new hole into your butt once. And she'll do it again, so you can put out more offal from your blasted body."

The undead pirate didn't flinch. "Oh, we see. Your beloved wife is here." He cackled. "Good. Her bleached skeleton will make for a good replacement to our prow's figurehead. You see, MacTavish is falling apart ... after all these years."

At that, Drake growled and produced his pistol, catching the fiend full in the stomach. The blow staggered the undead, but did not take him down.

"Kill them!" The Crimson Roger spat out the words like acidic venom. Immediately, the four undead enforcers, including Red Leg, moved quickly to comply. Each of the rotting creatures held a heavy cutlass easily in its grasp. Drake crossed his own blade with the undead captain, while his men joined the fray. Metal clashed against metal amid the sounds of chinking rings and chains, grunts from his men, and the quivering cannon fire in the distance. Drake heard a scream from somewhere in the dark but could not afford to look to see who had fallen. The Crimson Roger was a skilled fencer and Drake had to dig deep into his knowledge of swordplay to keep himself from ending impaled or chopped by Braziliano's cutlass. Another groan caught his ear, sign that the tireless sword arms of the Accursed had wounded another of his men.

"You'll join us soon," hissed the undead while thrusting forward. Drake dodged the blow and responded with a fast swing to the devil's head, but the Roger ducked, and then thrust again the blade toward his chest. At once, Drake caught the thrust and spun it wide, stepping in to slide his blade through the Crimson Roger's rib cage. The undead simply pulled himself free, seemingly unaffected by the wound, and came harder on his opponent just while one of the *Revenge*'s braves died under the cruel blades of the immortal Accursed. Through the clash of steel, Drake heard the last of cannon fire die away.

"You hear that?" Braziliano taunted. "That's the final shot that signals the death of your wife. Give up now, and we will allow her to return!"

Drake looked at the ugly, sunken features of what was once Geist and made his decision. "No, monster. I believe there's one other choice open to me. I can blast you out of this world and send you screaming into that evil *djab*'s arms that made you. See, I decided to find a *Bokor* meself. Seems *Ghede* gets very pissed at those crossing his plans. You killed the wrong woman, lad!" He latched the idol to the hilt of his cutlass. "I waged my soul I will stop you. Dead wife or not." He crouched down suddenly while the Crimson Roger's blade swung high above his head. 'And I will end you!"

Drake's weapon plunged deep into Braziliano's chest, impaling his unbeating heart. The undead staggered back, and Drake waited for the cold chill to fill his empty veins. The crystal skull fell out of the Roger's grip and thudded on the rocky floor. Then nothing.

Expecting something more, the Crimson Roger grinned. "You think this juju can stop us?"

The loud crack of a flintlock rifle shattered the crystal skull to pieces.

"Nay," Lorraine Dumont Davies replied from the cave's entrance. "But I bet that will do."

Immediately, a vaporous column of swirling mist escaped from the splintered figurine; grimy faces of cursed men, too long imprisoned into a horrible unlife, formed, then vanished in the billowing fog. The Accursed bodies crumpled to the floor and a terrible wail issued from the Crimson Roger's skeletal face. The fires died in his dead eyes, and then he collapsed like a puppet whose strings had been cut.

Drake looked around and realized that only his wife was there. None of his men had made it through the fight. But she was there, burned and bleeding. Yet alive.

He rushed to her and kissed her passionately. She responded with ardor, even if all her bones seemed to protest at the embrace. The kiss seemed to last forever.

Finally, they parted and he looked into her eyes. "How did you know? They said the skull couldn't be destroyed."

She grinned. "I didn't. I just thought no one had ever tried it. So ... why not?"

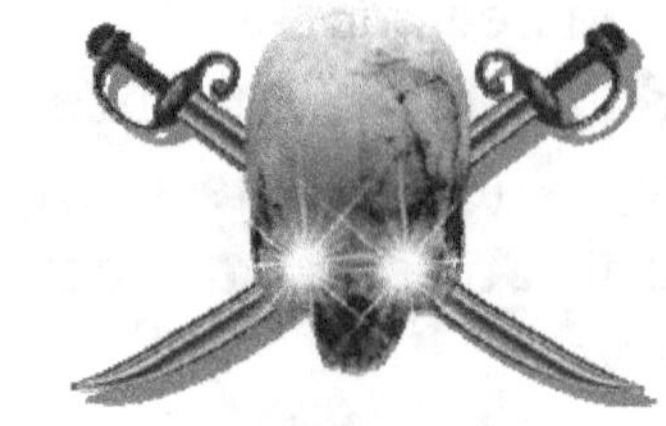

CHAPTER EIGHTEEN

OLD CAPTAINS NEVER DIE

While they left the cave, Drake asked his wife, "What about the *Raven's Nest*?"

She shook her head grimly, and then kept walking. With a sundered heart, Drake kept her pace, clutching her hand in a firm grip. This was their last adventure. From now on, the sea would be just a memory. It was time for a new generation of heroes to ply the waters.

Drake and Lorraine gazed out into the haze of the slowly receding fog and could just make out the crossbeam from a mainsail. Suddenly, a shout from the water could be heard.

"Ho, on the island! Captain Drake, are you there?" It was Higgins. The ship came into view as the fog melted away: she was battered and in sorry shape, but still afloat. They would need to stay on the island for a few days until she would be seaworthy again, but with the Crimson Roger gone, the spell seemed to be lifted from the isle.

Drake had done what he set out to do, and he had the evidence needed to prove that the *Black*

Brig was no more. The legend would live on for years to come and no one would ever really know what had happened on the little isle except for what was left of the *Revenge*'s crew. No one else would ever believe the story. It would just be another tall tale told in taverns and alehouses, another legend to tack.

Yet, Drake couldn't care. He had found his peace.

Finally.

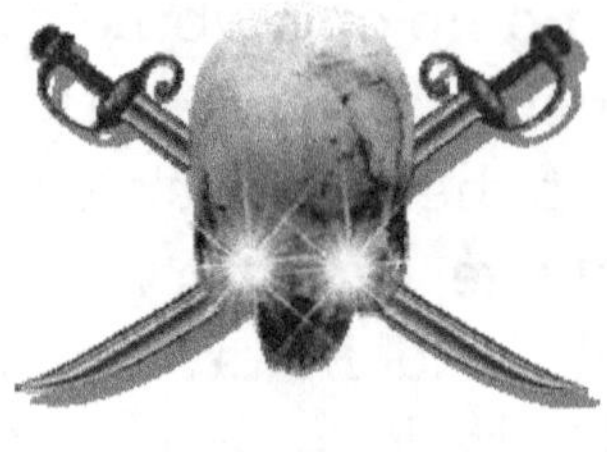

EPILOGUE

CURSE OF THE BLACK FLEET

Butcher's Bay, Crab Island. Nighttime.

The bay was awash with flotsam: fragmented memories of a bloody battle. Bloated bodies, or parts of them, bobbed on the surface of the calm sea, creating a bountiful banquet for aquatic creatures. Fishes of all size darted from frayed flesh to gruesome cavities, ignoring the larger predators. Those were too busy taking mouthful chunks out of the drifting buffet. The sea still reddened by the blood of many.

On the beach, a similar scene unfolded: flying scavengers hopped amidst pieces of men and jetsam. Mobs of crabs swarmed out of their hiding holes like spider rushing to a webbed prey, crawling on the top of one another eager to gorge on the sea's harvest. Flies and other insects were everywhere, filling the night with their constant buzzing.

Lying on the side, her hull marred by enormous holes, the wreck of the *Banshee's Cry* looked like the carcass of a beached whale. However, no scavenger dared to get too close, as if the animals sensed the taint of evil still surrounding that cursed ship. This vessel had been home of horrors for three decades, delivering death and despair whenever she had plunged anchor. And that taint still lingered, soaking her rotten wood from keel to topmast. Inside, the carnage mirrored the one on the beach. Yet, no varmint disturbed the dead flesh. The bodies lain sprawled amidst chunks of splintered hull, broken metal, and their decomposition fluids.

Except for the feeding frenzy happening in the waters and on the beach, the night stood still, as a lull had fallen on Crab Island: a testament to the world that a hurricane had finally died.

Suddenly, a vaporous mist began to seep out of the ship's putrid wood, slowly rising into the air and expanding at the same time into the bay, as if someone had started a fire inside the waterlogged husk, causing the trapped moisture to escape. At first, the scavengers ignored the fog, but as soon as it reached the floating bodies the fish swam away, alarmed. It took longer for the hungry sharks to abandon their bouncing dinner, yet, even they reluctantly left the scene when the mists grew denser.

When the vapors got hold of the land, all the varmint vanished, leaving the dead alone. The fog engulfed the bay, its tendrils snuck into the jungle, coating everything with moist. The landscape turned blurry and everything became an undistinguishable shadow.

With the animals gone, only death reigned on that land.

Then, a gloomy light came to life inside the mists. It was as if billions of phosphorescent organisms had taken home inside the vapors, and the glow gave the scenery an even eerier appearance. The luminescence was stronger around the human remains and it looked like it was emerging straight out of them. Inside the bay obscured by the fog, creaking sounds could be heard, and the more the mists coalesced, the more they grew in intensity. Sloshing sounds of things moving in the water, the clang of metal on wood, and the zipping twang of lines drawn taut. The fluttering of veils. And finally, the moans of something big stirring. It was like a hellish night shipyard.

The ship was rebuilding herself.

On the beach, in the jungle, in the waters, everywhere, the dead were shifting, as if coming out of a deep slumber. Severed hands scampered on the ground like grisly crabs looking for their home: their bodies. Dead eyes became alive and rolled inside their sockets. Drying innards slithered around like unholy snakes, and those whose bodies had been left in a better state lifted themselves from the sand – or the water – and slowly assumed an erect position. They stood where they arose, swaying, with no other purpose than waiting for the ship to call them back.

And, under the cold stars, that call came.

In the dark of the night, The *Black Brig* set sails with a full crew, heading fast, under a mysterious spell, toward a larger bank of fog.

There, the Black Fleet was waiting for her.

APPENDIX
Timeline
And
Pirate Glossary

TIMELINE
of the Dead Men Tell No Tales Universe

1508: The Black Fleet.

1519: Hernan Cortez and his men are slaughtered by the Aztecs.

1521: Pact of Blood between the Aztec Empire and the Kingdom of Spain.

1630: Tortuga in buccaneers' hands.

1649: Irish Revolt.

1662: Rock Braziliano captures a slaver ship.

1663: Birth of the Accursed.

1665: Mabouya's Curse.

1666: The Plague of London.

1667: Exodus to the New World.

1669: War of Unification. Northern Alliance (New England and Nouvelle France) against New Holland, Nueva Espana, the Free Colonies (Southern English Colonies), and the League of the Antilles.

1671: End of the Unification War.

1672: Drake becomes captain of the Banshee's Cry.

1673: All enemies of New Spain are branded as heretics by the Catholic Church. Lorraine Dumont becomes Le Corbeau Noir.

1674: Drake loses Harpy's Rock to Le Corbeau Noir.

1675: Nuevo Madrid established. The Banshee's Cry attacks Le Guisarme.

1676: End of Mabouya's Curse.

1677: Drake marries Lorraine Dumont and leaves the Account. Kaya's twins are born.

1680: Le Corbeau Noir returns to the Account.

1681: The Raven's Nest sinks.

1707: Kaya and her daughters slaughtered by the Black Brig.

1708: Battle of Crab Island.

PIRATE GLOSSARY
of the Dead Men Tell No Tales Universe

Ahoy! - a greeting, much like hello.

Affidavit - sworn oath to be truth. Also called Affy Davey.

Arrr! - yes, I agree. Hmm.

Articles - legal binding agreement. List of rules.

At Rope's End - another term for flogging.

Avast! - generally used as "hey!" Or a call for instant .attention.

Aye - yes (aye aye = yes, sir)

Belay - to stop an action, or to hold or secure.

Batten Down the Hatches - tie down the hatches. Also used as shut your mouth.

Bearings – location. To find where you are.

Bite the Bullet - be brave.

Black Spot - summons to a meeting, usually deadly.

Blaggards - aka blackguards. A scoundrel or jerk.

Blighter - a bad, gross person. .

Blimey! - an exclamation of surprise.

Bloody - damned or very good.

Bucko - generally means "friend", but can be used derisively as well.

Bungling - messing up, making mistakes.

Chase - pirates call the ship they are after the chase.

Cry Havoc - to start a war.

Davy Jones Locker - the bottom of the sea.

Dog Watch - late afternoon or early evening work shift.

Going on the Account - to become a pirate.

Grog - rum mixed with water.

Hand - to tie sails to the yardarms.

Hands - sailors.

Handsomely - gradually or slowly.

Have the Wind of - .to be in a better position than another person.

Heave - pull.

Hoist - to lift something.

Honest Air - sweet, pure air or not swampy.

Irons - handcuffs and shackles.

Jack Ketch – the hangman.

Jerked into the Devil's Arms - being hung.

Jolly Roger - pirate flag, usually has a skull and crossed bones.

Keelhauling - to drag a person across or along the keel of a ship, often fatal.

Landlubber – a land lover, not a sailor, or a wimpy person.

Leeward - or lee shore, the wind blows toward tis side, also a bad position.

Make Sail - unroll and put sail down. Also to set course.

Make Terms - agree to rules.

Maroon - abandon on a deserted island.

Matey - also mate, another sailor on the ship who is a friend.

Me - pirates use this instead of 'my', they also use it for 'me'.

Parley - discussion between enemies.

Quartermaster - officer in charge of assigning rooms and supplies.

Sail Ho! - a call to let the crew know that a ship has been spotted on the horizon, since the sail is usually the first thing seen.

Scurvy Dog - derogatory term for a bad or no good pirate.

Sealegs - ability to walk steadily on the deck of a moving ship.

Shiver Me Timbers - Scary, makes my bones shake.

Sink Me! - another colorful expression.

Smart as Paint - smart, fresh, new, honest.

Smartly - quickly.

Square - fair, honest.

Steer - to guide a ship by using its rudder and ship's wheel.

Swab - a disrespectful term for a pirate, called so because those with the task of swabbing or scrubbing the deck are usually put there in punishment.

Tall Ship - any ship with tall masts.

Trim Sail - adjust the sails.

ABOUT
JEFFREY KOSH

Jeffrey Kosh is the author of three novels, some novelettes, and a long series of short stories. Perhaps best known for his horror fiction, Jeffrey also writes erotica and likes to experience different paths. His works have been published by Alexandria Publishing Group, Grinning Skull Press, May-December Publications, Optimus Maximus Publishing, and EFW.

He is the owner of Jeffrey Kosh Graphics where he creates book covers for various authors and publishing companies, movie posters and DVD jackets. His various careers have led him to travel extensively worldwide, developing a passion for cinema, wildlife, history, and popular folklore.

All these things heavy influences his writing style.

BIBILOGRAPHY

FEEDING THE URGE - Novel
DEAD MEN TELL NO TALES - Novel
THE HAUNTER OF THE MOOR. - Novel
SPIRITS AND THOUGHT FORMS, Tales from Prosperity Wells. – Short Stories Collection
TALES FROM THE DEAD – Short Stories Collection
THRILL OF THE HUNT – Novelette
HOME INVASION - Novelette

Grinning Skull Press
P.O. Box 67
Bridgewater, MA 02324
e-mail: support@grinningskullpress.com

www.grinningskullpress.wordpress.com